I0667424

RIVER STONE

A Novel
by JB Winsor

Boulder Digital Publishing, LLC
Boulder, Colorado

ISBN 978-0-9829194-1-5
Copyright 2011 by JB Winsor

Published by Boulder Digital Publishing, LLC
Boulder, Colorado

Also by JB Winsor

Love of the Hunt

Short Stories available on:

Amazon Kindle:
The Wolf

jbwinsor.com:
Senior Prom
The Lover
Fishing Down a Manhole

RIVER STONE

Chapter 1

Manhattan

"Dead."

The word reverberated inside Justin Thatcher's skull, as loud as if he had been standing next to the great carillon bells in the tower of the Riverside Church, repetitive shock waves of a death knell battering him with an intensity that curiously filled him with sadness and joy, with guilt and elation. He leaned back in his desk chair, rubbing his temples, turning permutations of the word over and over in his mind: dying, die, death, dead.

It was over. He could move on.

Looking for patterns that might quell emotions triggered by the telephone call, he searched the Oriental rug on his office floor, the two Renoirs displayed against walnut paneling and, on the other wall, the forty-nine silver framed "tombstones" announcing his business triumphs. The rich scents of his office, those barely perceptible odors of wood, wool and paper, those once reassuring scents that anchored him to a familiar and safe world, now spoke of death.

He fished the river stone from his pocket and rubbed its smooth patina. He remembered that evening before leaving the ranch twenty-eight years ago. He had walked the riverbank below the cabin to avoid another argument. Sunlight had angled low from behind shadowed mountain peaks, penetrating the river's blue waters, highlighting the stone. Intrigued by its color, he'd plucked it from the ice-cold river. He'd studied the stone, turning it in the sun's last rays, watching the subtle change in the stone's color, fingers caressing its smooth surface. He'd slipped the river stone into his pocket as a reminder to never return, hoping it would become a talisman to protect him from the memories of that place.

And he remembered the next morning, walking down the cabin steps and past the dreaded shed with his belongings packed in a black cardboard suitcase, watching his old man rake up fresh horse manure between the cabin and Old Tan where Cody sat behind the steering wheel to drive him to the bus stop. Blocking his way for one last confrontation. Arguing. Showing his father the stone, saying it would be a reminder to never return. That's what triggered what had happened next.

He shook that memory from his head and thought about what Cody had said about their father's death — a suspicious accident.

Even so, Justin told his brother he would not return for the funeral. After twenty-eight years, he would not break his vow.

He heard laughter from his assistant's office: a man and woman, happy sounds, a bitter contrast to his brother's voice announcing their father's death, the laughter a reminder that life moves on, a reminder of the insignificance of one person's life within the grand scheme of things.

It was during the second phone call, the conversation with the attorney in Montana, when he agreed to go back, but he didn't tell Cody. He felt both responsible for tending to things, but at the same time surprisingly free of having to take care of anything at all. How could he explain that to Cody?

His assistant appeared in his doorway and said it was time for the meeting. A few minutes later, surrounded by associates and assistants, he sat at the conference room table across from

8

three men who represented a buyer for one of the companies he controlled. He touched the river stone in his pocket for good luck as he pretended to read a thick sale document while he watched the men through his peripheral vision. Like predators before a kill, they leaned forward, watched and waited.

The words on the document blurred as his mind returned to the phone call. Even after all those years of silence, he'd recognized Cody's voice, tinged with apprehension and emotion. Their father gone, carrying away the nightmares, he hoped.

He flipped to the signature page, reached into his suit pocket and pulled out a fountain pen engraved with his initials. The men glanced at each other and grinned, predators about to become prey.

He put the pen down, flipped back a page, and then read a paragraph about the seller's representations and warrants. The buyers glanced at each other. He asked them to explain a clause. The lawyer began to justify the language in a rush of complex words and sentences that everyone in the room knew was elegant bullshit. That's why he earned a thousand bucks an hour. Carried by the torrent of words, the stench of his cigar breath spewed across the table. He could smell the lawyer's sour fear of losing the deal.

Justin loved this part of a negotiation, loved playing with buyers like a cat with a mouse. He felt he was different than most he dealt with, those self-proclaimed hot shots who constantly hustled, talked too much and played every angle to the point of dishonesty. He didn't like to waste words. He prided himself on being honest. He wasn't out to screw his opponents. On the other hand, he didn't feel obligated to stop them from screwing themselves. Nodding agreement, he picked up the fountain pen with his right hand and then used his thumb and forefinger to twist off the cap. He dropped the cap on the table, the sound sharp. The predators exchanged glances. When he lowered the pen toward the signature line, the attorney leaned forward, elbows on the table. Justin raised the pen and heard them hold their breath. He smiled and then signed the sale agreement.

The buyers exhaled. They laughed. They high-fived. One muttered, "Gotcha!"

Justin slid the document across the table to the leader, who checked Justin's signature and then gloated. "You had no idea how valuable that company was."

Justin stood and buttoned his coat. "I'm glad you're happy. So am I. You just paid seventy million more than anyone else offered."

Their smiles died.

"It was good to do business with you, gentlemen. My assistant will show you out." Justin walked from the conference room to his office. His ex-father-in-law and senior partner Thomas Farnsworth, a silver-haired man with a patrician face, waited for him.

"Close the deal?"

"Yes," Justin said. "It's finished."

The smile faded from Farnsworth's face as the full implication sank in. "Now you'll have enough fees to pay off your loan."

"Just before your usurious penalty clause would have kicked in."

"I wouldn't have enforced it."

"Of course not," Justin said.

"Do you plan to stay?"

"We'll talk about that when I get back from my trip."

The right corner of Farnsworth's mouth twitched, the fleeting tic that appeared when he lost, a rare event. He nodded and then walked out of Justin's office.

Justin could add another silver framed tombstone that announced this last deal, now fifty. Each one held a story of a special tactic he had utilized. The first time he had walked into this office, he had felt intimidated. Now this was his home. And now that his fees could pay off Farnsworth's loan, he would no longer have to serve the man like an indentured servant. He would be free. And yet the implications of his father's death cast a pall over this most recent victory.

In his private bathroom, he stripped off his shirt, washed his upper body and then rolled on deodorant. He opened his closet and counted the new shirts hanging from the bar. His assistant would have to order two dozen more. He took a shirt from the hanger, raised its fabric to his nose and inhaled its fresh starchiness. That scent reminded him how far he'd come. Everything would be all right. He smiled, slipped on the shirt and then buttoned it up.

A few minutes later, Justin's assistant walked into his office and told him there was an emergency. Ashley demanded they meet at once. He swore under his breath. Everything with Ashley was an emergency. He told his assistant to push back his next appointment one hour.

He arrived at the Harvard Club, surprised to see their eleven-year-old son with Ashley. William, wearing his school blazer, should have been at Collegiate. As always, Ashley looked perfect. She glanced at her watch, shook her head and then, without a word, marched to the center of the deserted Hall, orchestrating one of her drama-queen scenes he knew only too well.

They followed her. William had once told him Harvard Hall, with the elephant's head protruding from the wall, ears spread wide, trunk extended, and the room's three-story ceiling, dark beams, and molding-hung tapestries, looked like Harry Potter's Hogwart's School. Now he saw it the same way.

Still in full drama-queen mode, she sat in the middle of a red tufted leather couch, arranging herself, back rigid, legs crossed, fingers laced, forcing him to sit on an opposing couch next to William. His son shook the bangs away from his eyes, looked at his mother and then at him. Justin couldn't read anything in his look — a pure blank slate. The boy scooted back in the deep seat, and then jammed his heels on the edge.

"Take your feet off the seat," he said.

William slouched and then swung his feet back and forth, heels bumping against the leather.

Justin gritted his teeth — now was not the time to push the boy further. William began playing a video game on his portable player.

Ashley's hair was perfect, the result of a daily session with her personal stylist. She favored outfits by top designers who personally draped her slim figure. She kept her hemlines a bit shorter than current fashion to show off her legs. She wore matching bright multi-colored high heels.

Justin thought of her shoes as her "fuck-me pumps." When men looked her over, he'd noticed, their eyes started with the shoes, slithered up her legs and under her skirt to an imagined moist nirvana, except that he knew she was a cold bitch, in bed and out.

But that was harsh. Those were the things that first attracted him. The girls where he grew up sometimes combed their hair back into a ponytail, not for looks but utility — to keep it out of the way when they did chores, rode or roped. There, Wranglers were women's standard fare, starched when they dressed up. Worlds apart. He suspected he'd been an innocent on her playing field.

Ashley had been schooled in the feminine graces and she was an expert at turning on the charm — like that Thanksgiving when her brother invited him from Harvard to spend the holiday weekend. Shortly after they were introduced, she decided she wanted Justin. She applied a full court press of charm that made her sexy and warm like a bonfire is warm, always making him gauge how close to get.

He wasn't sure if he'd fallen in love with her or her manicured guise — either way, he'd fallen hard. He had also been impressed that her father, Thomas Farnsworth, owned the oldest family investment firm on Wall Street. Marriage hadn't been what either one expected. Ashley had asked for the divorce and he hadn't fought it. He had continued to work with Farnsworth, who valued a moneymaking junior partner more than a son-in-law.

Sometimes he missed having her accompany him to charity events — a woman who looked perfect and acted gracious — but other times like this, when she acted imperious and judgmental, he couldn't stand to be near her.

Ashley poised on the edge of the couch, foot pumping. She smiled her tight-lipped little way and said, "I've been promoted to head the International Division of Lightner Advertising."

"That's wonderful," he said, and he meant it. Even during their marriage, she'd always wanted to prove to her father that she could be a "Farnsworth" type of businessperson.

Her smile turned serious. "My promotion means I'll be traveling most of the time. I'm opening an office in London. William will have to stay with you all summer, at least."

"No problem, he's enrolled in summer camp."

William cut him an alarmed glance.

Ashley's lips formed her I'm-so-sorry smile.

"I have one more bit of news about *your* son."

William was *her* son when he did something she could brag about. Justin braced himself.

The boy's thumbs stopped tapping.

Ashley leaned forward as if the empty Hall had ears. It was not unlike the first time they'd kissed, she moving in with a determined, now in retrospect, conquering expression on her face, lips parting. But this time instead of the thrill of a mouth to explore, she spoke. "*Your* son has been expelled from Collegiate!"

"Expelled?" He looked at William. The boy stared across the hall at a massive fireplace.

"And from the school's summer camp!"

"Why?"

"He made a bomb."

Justin turned to the boy. "A bomb?"

William retreated to the video game.

Ashley continued, "The headmaster evacuated the school and called the police. A SWAT team and bomb disposal squad swooped down upon them. William was accused and expelled. It will be so embarrassing for me."

"I can't take him," Justin said.

"What?" she asked.

"I'm going to Cora in the morning."

Her laugh became hysterical. "Don't tell me you're going to break your promise never to go back? Your father won."

"My father died."

"Oh! I can picture it now. The grieving son." She laughed again. "There must be money involved."

He felt his jaw twitch.

"William will enjoy seeing where you grew up." She looked at her watch and stood up. "If I don't hurry, I'll be late for my mani-pedi. I'll have to drop William off at my place so he can pack. Juanita will take him to your condo. He'll be there when you get home from the party tonight. See you there."

No doubt about it, the woman had bitch down to an art. Worst of all, she always got what she wanted. He might as well have not been in the conversation. He sat there like a fool watching her march out of Harvard Hall with William in tow.

Much later that night, Justin opened his eyes and stared into a void as black as the inside of a buried casket. He listened to his ragged breathing and the distant wail of a siren as he struggled to quell his rising panic at not being sure where he was.

There was a burst of red light. He tried to discern anything solid to anchor himself to reality. The light went out and his world plunged into black. Three seconds later, the light flooded back. A reddish glow and then a black void, on and off, red and black, black and red, a rhythm that matched his heartbeat.

His eyes began to focus.

A beam of light burst through a gap in closed drapes. He made out the corner of a ceiling and a dresser. A fractured face stared at him — a grotesque Dali print. This was no place that he knew, had ever known.

The room dropped into a black void that conjured up voices from the past, each a strand of a spider's silk sticking to him until he was trapped in its web, about to be dragged back to that god-forsaken place.

Seconds later, another spurt of light revealed tangled clothes strewn across the floor — a tuxedo shirt, bow tie, pants, and, near the door, a woman's black thong tangled in a high heeled shoe.

During the next blackout, splintered memories flooded his mind. His mother's eyes staring at him through a hole she'd wiped in the frost on the window above the kitchen sink. Her disappearing. The shed. His father.

Relief and regret pulsed with the reddish neon glow blinking outside the window, feeding his loneliness.

The next beam of light revealed a bed sheet crumpled against the footboard. Next to him, a woman lay on her back, snoring softly. Her lips quivered as she exhaled night breath. The neon glow made her red hair look black. Pyramid-shaped nipples topped cantaloupe-hard breasts. He wondered what they had looked like before surgery.

He inhaled her scent, a blend of dried sweat and stale perfume. As with all the others, even Ashley, he knew, maybe had always known, something was wrong, that she was wrong, that she smelled wrong, that she moved wrong and tasted wrong. He could never stop comparing the way it was with other women to the way it had been with his first love, but perhaps she had become a fantasy created by a long-ago memory.

The woman's snoring grew louder. He could not remember

her name. He struggled to gather the right facts. This afternoon Ashley had chained an anchor to his leg, a burden he would have to drag with him tomorrow when he returned to his childhood home — if home was the right word. And then, at the MOMA charity dinner, Ashley had introduced him to this woman. He shook his head now at the irony of it all. After all these years, the marriage, the child, everything, he hadn't a clue as to what ran Ashley's chilly heart.

He now remembered he had called the woman "Red." She hadn't objected. He didn't want to know her real name, didn't want to go through the pretense of exchanging cell numbers, didn't want to play the two-faced game of saying it had been great, he'd call soon. He wanted to flee.

He slipped out of bed, picked up his clothes, dressed and then tiptoed out the door. He took the elevator down to the lobby and pushed through the door into cold air laced with a faint sewer stench. Steam rose from sidewalk grates, lost souls rising into the night.

He walked through shadows, heels striking a sharp sound that echoed hollow from brick walls. He turned the corner into the pulsing neon light. He looked at an electric billboard mounted high on the wall of a Salvation Army building that hummed: JESUS SAVES.

He watched the sign blink on and off: JESUS SAVES. JESUS SAVES.

He stared at Red's seventh floor window and then at the pulsing sign. He felt lonelier than ever before. He touched the river stone in his pocket.

Washed by the blood red light, he spread his arms wide as if nailed to a cross, lowered his head and prayed — something he didn't do often. He waited. Nothing.

He glanced at his watch — nearly two in the morning. He had to get back to the condo, where his son would still be up, playing his damned computer games. He needed to get the boy to bed, pack their suitcases and then try to get some sleep. He ran his fingers through his hair, not sure why he'd chosen this night to do this, this night before going back to where it had begun. He pulled up his collar, jammed his hands in his pockets and shuffled through an empty night.

Chapter 2

Early the next morning, Justin and William stood on the sidewalk outside his 28th floor condo in the Sherry-Netherland on 59th and 5th, waiting for a limo. They were dressed alike in khakis, sport coats and open-collared white shirts. The boy stared through sandy bangs at the screen of his game player, thumbs tapping a furious pace against the keyboard, lost as usual in a video game. Now that Ashley was leaving for Europe, William was his and he had to take the kid back with him. Troubles came in bunches.

William said something to him.

"What?" He regretted the irritated edge to his voice.

"Nothing."

"What do you want?"

"I don't want to go. Do I have to?"

"If you hadn't gotten expelled, you wouldn't have to go, would you?"

The corner of the boy's lip curled upward in a dismissive way and then he returned to the game on his iPad. Justin had no idea what to do with his son – especially after the disaster at school.

Justin paced next to the four-foot clock perched atop a fluted column and then glanced up the street for the limo.

The damn driver was late. Every time Justin turned he

either saw William engrossed in his game or the clock moving ever-so-quickly forward. The limo was to take them to the Teterboro airport to fly more than two thousand miles west to Missoula, the closest airport to Cora and the ranch. He dreaded going back. He looked at his watch and then at Alex, the Sherry-Netherland's doorman.

"It's coming, Mr. Thatcher."

Alex had been staring at William. It wasn't often the boy was with Justin, and the doorman, like a keen eyed hunter, could tell arrangements had changed. They had, and Justin's life would be more complicated now.

A blasting horn – a taxi driver, impatient to move when the light changed, gave a motorist hell. Justin looked in vain for his limo.

"Yes!" William said.

"What?"

"I just beat level nine," the boy said without taking his eyes off his iPad.

"That's just great."

William returned to his game.

Across the street, on the edge of Central Park, a squirrel scampered down the trunk of a maple tree and scurried across the sidewalk. It paused at the curb, tail flicking as it watched traffic, waiting for the light to change. The squirrel looked into Justin's eyes as if asking permission to cross. Justin felt himself tense.

The animal leaped into the street and scurried past still tires and then under a tourist bus. The light changed. Traffic spurted forward. The squirrel froze amid the spinning wheels of machines rushing past and then made its decision. It hopped toward Justin, tail high. Justin saw the car and felt himself twist, knowing what was going to happen. A sedan's front left tire crushed the little animal flat. And then the back tire thumped over the body. Its tail rose from the blacktop like a quivering exclamation point.

William's laughter edged up at him.

"What are you laughing at?"

William nodded toward the carcass. "Looks like someone lost at Frogger."

"Don't you have any damned feelings?"

"For what, a stupid squirrel that runs across the street?"

Justin clenched his fists. His father would have done a lot more than clench his fists. His dead father. He watched his son return to the video game. William acted as though the squirrel's death was nothing more than a scene from one of his digital games, not knowing which was reality, not caring.

It was more than a lack of respect that bothered Justin – his son didn't understand social graces, the common thoughtfulness that allowed one to move through the world, the consideration that helps others give you what you want and what you need. William seemed to specialize in not getting what he wanted.

Justin looked at the little body of the squirrel in the street and a pain shot through his chest. What dignity was there in being crushed to death between rubber and asphalt?

The doorman moved up beside him.

"Did you see what happened?" he asked Alex.

"Feed him every day. I'll miss him," the doorman pulled a peanut from his pocket, a single one on his open palm, and then Justin understood – the squirrel hadn't been coming to him, it was crossing the street for a peanut. For some reason, that made him feel sadder.

He slipped Alex a twenty.

"Would you take his body over to the Park and bury it someplace?"

"Yes sir. Better than rotting in the street."

The doorman opened a closet and found a long-handled pan used for picking up cigarette butts. He waited for traffic to stop for a red light, walked onto the street, scraped the squirrel's body into the pan with the side of his shoe and then hid the pan in the corner by the revolving doors. The dead squirrel's bushy tail protruded.

"I'll bury him on break."

William rolled his eyes. "Nobody buries squirrels."

Justin clamped his jaw.

William returned to his game.

The limo arrived and the driver popped the trunk open. The doorman picked up William's overnight suitcase and put it in. Next to it, he tossed Justin's suitcase, containing starched shirts, two pair of boxer shorts and two pairs of socks. Eight new shirts should be enough for a three-day trip.

Chapter 3

Several minutes later, the limo merged with traffic stream-ing toward the Lincoln Tunnel. They sat in the back seat, alone, silent, staring at the reflections of grimy buildings sliding past. During the drive, Justin wondered what William thought of him as a father. His own old man had been a terrible father. The boy had no idea how lucky he was.

Twelve miles later, at the airport, they checked in at the pas-senger desk of Atlantic Aviation before being ushered onto the tarmac where they walked through the pungent odor of jet fuel toward a waiting Cessna Citation X.

The jet's sensuous fuselage with the enormous air intakes in front of its radically sweptback wings made it the world's fast-est civilian aircraft. Even though he didn't own it, Justin took a large amount of pride in that plane. It was Farnsworth's jet, built for work. Justin had crossed the country several times in it, head buried in work papers.

"We'll be flying faster than commercial jets. About seven hundred miles-per-hour," Justin said.

"Whatever."

William was as accustomed to flying on a private jet as Jus-tin had been to riding horses as a kid. He wondered if the two experiences were that different. Deep down he knew they were — you were never totally in control of a twelve-hundred-pound horse — anything could happen, like the time a horse he was riding had stepped on a hornet's nest and bucked him off. Planes were safer.

The cabin smelled of leather, like a new luxury car. There was a small conference table in the front corner near the cockpit. Tan leather seats occupied each side of the twenty-four-foot-long aisle.

The co-pilot stowed their bags and asked them to take a seat. Justin let William choose his seat first — otherwise the boy would have distanced himself as far as possible. It was a dance they played, in restaurants, theaters, whenever they were together. William flopped into a seat and stared out the window. Justin sat across the aisle.

"Buckle up, son."

"There's more work space up front. Why don't you sit up there?" William asked with tight lips.

Those lips came from Ashley, and although she was an undeniably beautiful woman, he'd come to despise the angles that defined that beauty. It was hard to see them on his son. As he tried to do with Ashley, Justin ignored him and stayed put.

Several minutes later, the jet rolled into position on their assigned runway. The pilot jammed the throttle to the firewall. The plane shuddered and then shot ahead. Gravity slammed William deep into the seat. The boy looked at the ceiling, eyes bright. His lips trembled and then he almost smiled. Justin remembered seeing that look on William when he was five and had righted himself on a two-wheeler. In this, he could see his son's love of a thrill, a challenge, and he felt that under all those layers of his mother's DNA of disdain there was something of him in William.

Justin closed his eyes and felt the power of the jet engines propelling them to Montana. The fastest transportation at the ranch had been Old Tan, the ancient truck that was grouchy as an old lady wracked by rheumatism.

In no time, the jet reached an altitude of 42,000 feet above a solid cloud deck. William played the video game, the tapping of his thumbs a counterpoint to the sound of the engines.

Justin drifted into his adult concerns. He'd been suffocating under a mountain of debt from the failed internet IPO, the divorce and their lifestyle. That had changed, now that he had closed this last deal. After paying off Farnsworth, he would be free to leave with the equity he'd earned. That would be enough for a luxurious retirement, but he wanted more. That opportunity had presented itself last week when Brad Duncan, chairman of the world's largest private equity firm, invited him to join as a senior partner and promised he'd have a shot at the chairmanship.

Justin pressed his forehead against the plane's window and watched clouds billow upward with explosive fury. Justin turned toward his son, still engrossed in the video game.

"Let's talk about the bomb."

The kid's thumbs didn't falter. "Let's not."

Justin reached across the aisle, grabbed the game and put it on his lap. "What *do* you want to talk about?"

"I want my game back!"

"After we talk."

The boy folded his arms across his chest and glared out the window.

Justin jammed the iPad in the seat pocket. If this were a test of William's patience, Justin would win. Years of negotiating had given him more than enough experience to out-wait an eleven-year-old addicted to video games. He leaned back, closed his eyes and waited.

He had assigned his assistant the impossible task of finding another summer camp. Most were booked years in advance. He told her to offer a generous bonus for a last-minute acceptance. Money talked, but apparently not this time. The private system was tight; one phone call to his school revealed the bomb incident, and no one in a post-9/11 world wanted to accept the boy. His last assignment for his secretary had been to find a boarding school.

Justin heard a gagging sound. William held his hands over his mouth.

"What's wrong?" Justin asked.

"I throw up on planes unless I can concentrate on a video game," the boy muttered between his fingers.

Justin watched him gag and couldn't tell if he was telling the truth or pretending. If this were a power play, the kid would threaten to throw up every time he didn't get his way. He realized he didn't know his son very well. If he had pulled a stunt like that when he was William's age, his old man would have laughed and said, "Fine. Who cares?"

William gagged louder.

He had the choice of giving in or taking the risk of flying the rest of the way with puke smell.

"Okay, I believe you get sick on planes, but don't try to pull that trick anywhere else." He gave William the iPad.

The boy made a miraculous recovery.

Chapter 4

When the jet touched down on the runway in Missoula, Justin reset his watch from Eastern to the Mountain time zone. They had gained two hours. Now 9:30, there was more than enough time to get to the funeral. The pilot taxied to the terminal, parked and shut down the engines. The co-pilot opened the fuselage door. Crisp mountain air flooded into the cabin. Justin smiled – he'd forgotten the smell of clean air.

He rented a car, bought sandwiches and pop to go, and then they drove toward Cora. A half hour later, William fell asleep. Justin turned onto an empty blacktop under an intense blue sky and sped through country filled with sagebrush, bunch grass and Black Angus. He lowered his window and smelled the bitter-pleasant fragrance of sage, an almost forgotten scent. Later, the boy woke up and reached for his iPad.

"This would be a good time to talk about school and the bomb."

"I don't want to talk about it." William thumbed his game.

Justin counted the highway center stripes. After he'd counted two hundred, he said, "Put it down. We need to talk."

"Not!"

Impaled on the barbed wire of fences lining both sides of the road, white plastic grocery sacks fluttered like handkerchiefs. Windblown tumbleweeds jammed against the fences. He slammed on the brakes. The car veered and then skidded to a halt.

"Okay." William put the game in the back seat and Justin pulled back onto the road.

As they accelerated, a tumbleweed bounced across the pavement, and shattered on the front grill, showering brittle pieces over the hood and against the windshield.

The boy whooped. "Hit another."

Three minutes later he spotted a huge weed tumbling across a field far ahead. "See that one off to the right? Bet I can hit it."

"Not. The fence will stop it first."

"I hit it, you talk."

The boy looked at him for a long moment. "Yokay."

He slowed, timing his speed to intercept the tumbleweed.

William leaned forward. "It won't get over the fence."

The weed hung on the barbed wire and then a gust of wind lifted it up and over onto the road's shoulder. Justin tightened his grip on the wheel and floored the gas pedal. The car spurted forward. There was no traffic on the long straight stretch. The weed tumbled across their lane. He swerved into the oncoming lane and onto the far shoulder and smashed into the tumbleweed. It shattered into hundreds of needles that reflected sunlight as they ricocheted off the windshield like hail. William flinched.

The right front tire hooked the pavement and the car's left tires rose as it spun a three-sixty across the blacktop. He fought the steering wheel and skidded the car into the road, going sixty.

William's arms were braced against the dash, face white. "That was sick!"

He kicked the speed up to seventy and a few silent miles later smashed another tumbleweed. He waited for the boy to live up to his end of the bargain.

"Who taught you to do that?" William asked.

"Who taught you to make a confetti bomb?"

"Googled it."

"Can't Google how to smash tumbleweeds."

"You sure?"

Justin shrugged. "So tell me how you made it?"

"Just followed the web page instructions."

"Enlighten me."

"I got some film canisters from a picture processing place and found a can of that stuff used to blow dust off of computers and then I scooped up a couple handfuls of those paper dots from the hole punch they use at school," William said, becoming more animated. "Then all I had to do was turn the air duster can upside down and squirt some liquid into the canister. I filled it with confetti and then snapped on the canister lid tight. It takes anywhere from five seconds to a minute to explode. It's really cool."

"Any particular reason you felt like doing that?"

William's words gushed out. "This kid with a locker next to me is a big bully. He'd been picking on me, so I took the stuff to my locker and made the confetti bomb and put it on top of his locker just before he opened it up. He shoved me out of the way, like always, and the bomb went off and he got paper holes all over his head and when everyone was laughing and watching him brush the paper out of his hair, I stuck the big bomb inside his locker."

He cut a look at his son. "Big bomb?"

"You didn't think they'd kick me out for a little confetti explosion, did you?"

He took his foot off the pedal and let the car slow. "So, how'd you learn how to make that big bomb?"

"I just used my imagination. I got this old tin box and I bought a stolen cell phone . . ."

"You bought a stolen cell phone?"

"Sure, you can buy stuff like that from people on the street."

"How much?"

"Twenty. I downloaded a bomb ring-tone for the phone, set the answer for the maximum rings, put it inside the box. And then I taped two batteries with snap-on connectors on the top of the box, punched a hole and ran red wires from the batteries into the box. It was pretty simple."

"Let me see if I have this figured out. It looked like a bomb and sounded like a bomb, but it was fake."

"What, you think I wanted to kill someone? I just wanted to see him shit himself."

"Watch your language. OK, so when everyone was looking at the bully, you hid the fake bomb inside his locker. And then what happened?"

"I didn't think anyone saw me put it there and I was going to call to make the ring-tone go 'bang' the next time the asshole opened his locker."

"Language."

"Yeah. So I was in class when the fire bell rang and we were herded outside. Then the SWAT team and bomb guys arrived. When they were inside, I thought it would be fun to use my cell phone and call the phone in the locker."

"Is that when you were caught?"

"Everybody was calling their parents, so no one noticed me."

"How did they catch you?"

"They said the bomb guys were opening the locker when I called and the phone ring-tone went off – Bang! I guess that really scared them, because they were really pissed off."

"Watch your language. So how did they catch you?"

"Some girl saw me hide the bomb in the bully's locker and she squealed. They didn't see anything funny about it and they didn't care if I was getting even."

"Some adults have no sense of humor."

"Yeah, but a lot of the kids think I'm a hero."

"What do you think?"

"Maybe it went too far."

"Got to agree. And now we're stuck with each other."

"You got that right," the boy said.

He drove for several miles, thinking about the incident and how he should react. His old man wouldn't have had to think about reacting. It would have been shed-time.

"Sometimes bullies need to be taken down a notch, but why didn't you talk to me about the problem?" Justin asked.

"You wouldn't have cared," the boy said with a new tone to his voice.

"Of course I would have."

"Haven't before."

"That's not true," Justin said, but he knew how the boy could feel that way. He'd been so busy.

"You didn't come to my birthday party."

That was true, but he was terrible about remembering dates and Ashley, in her typical passive-aggressive behavior, hadn't told him about the party. She loved making him look bad.

"I meant to be there, but I put it my schedule for the next day," he lied.

"You don't care about me. Mom doesn't care about me, either. She left you. Now she's leaving me." He began to cry.

He thought about pulling over and holding him, but the boy was too old — he'd never been hugged at William's age. Better to reason with him.

"Your mother hasn't abandoned you."

"She has."

He didn't know what else to say. "It's not the end of the world. It'll be okay, son."

"No . . . it . . . won't. It won't be the same, ever."

Justin knew he was right. What's more, there was something about his son's sobbing gasps for breath that tore at him. Justin finally recognized the sound — it had the same feel as the wind howling through cracks in the window frame next to his bed on lonely winter nights after his mother had disappeared.

Chapter 5

An hour later, Justin pulled to the crest of the hill overlooking a small town nestled against a mountain range. He touched his river stone and then looked at his watch. They had plenty of time before the service.

The boy looked up from his video game. "Why'd we stop?"

"That's my home town."

"Looks like a microchip."

Even from this distance the town had a straight-line, never-grown look. Everything was uniform, even the height of the trees rising above the flat valley. A wide ribbon of irrigated green fields spread from both sides of the river that began high in the far mountains, ran through town and then snaked through sagebrush flats. Justin could see the boy's point. The town had the symmetry of some small piece of electronic machinery, old and outdated, a transistor more than a chip, but solid.

"Is that where the funeral is?" the boy asked.

"Yes."

"I've never been to one. You go to lots?"

"Not here. Haven't been here in twenty-eight years."

That was the truth — technically speaking — he hadn't been back to Cora. Fifteen years earlier, resolved to confront his father, he'd flown to Missoula, rented a car, driven to this exact spot, pulled off, looked at the town and sat several hours before he lost his nerve. He turned around and flew back to Manhattan.

"Where's the ranch?"

"About forty miles from town, beyond that lowest spot on the ridgeline."

He pointed to a mountain range north of Cora and traced the line of the dirt road that snaked up from the valley to the mountain pass that he'd driven over every day with Cody to school, when a snowstorm didn't strand them for several days in town or worse, strand them at the ranch with the old man.

"I want to see it," William said.

"We don't have time on this trip." If he played the estate business right, he'd never have to come back to Cora, much less go to the damned ranch.

"Why don't you want to go home?"

He'd never considered the ranch a home, not since his mother disappeared. "I told you. We don't have time."

"Why didn't you come back to see your Dad when he was alive?"

"We . . . it's complicated."

"Mom says you're just like him," the boy said.

Justin's jaw twitched. "Your Mom never met my father."

"Whatever."

"You're too young to understand."

"Yeah."

"Time to eat." He handed William a sandwich and pop.

"Why don't we eat down there?"

"Because this is more efficient." He dreaded having to confront his brother and the rest of the locals, but he was on a mission — settle the damned estate business, talk to Miss Adams, his teacher, and then get the hell out of town.

They ate in silence. A few minutes later, he got out of the car, opened the trunk, unzipped his suitcase and put on a clean shirt.

On the outskirts of town, they drove past a dilapidated motel with a torn cardboard "Open" sign in the window. Old snow-mobiles and a pickup with a flat tire lay in front. Several hundred yards later, a ramshackle café leaned windward. A quarter mile further there was a new roadside billboard:

Cora, Montana - Home of
Little League State Champions
2007, 2008, 2009

A picture of Coach Billy Baxter smiled at them. Justin smiled back. Billy had been a star athlete, attracted girls like bees to honey and initiated practical jokes for others to pull — and for others to take the punishment when caught. Justin had been caught several times, but he didn't mind – Billy created a buzz of excitement, something lacking from ranch life.

They had been best friends until spring of their senior year when Billy heard Justin won the scholarship to Harvard. Billy stopped talking to him and told anyone who would listen that Justin thought he was too good for his old friends and that he'd never return.

On that summer day at the bus stop, Billy watched from across the street. Justin boarded the bus and took a seat. Through the dirty window, he gave Billy their old friendship sign – pointing the fist like a pistol, index finger barrel, thumb hammer-cocked and then the upward jerk mimicking the recoil of a shot. Billy flipped him the finger, spat a hawker for good riddance and walked away. Justin re-lived that scene, over and over, all the way across country, wondering why his best friend couldn't feel happy for Justin's opportunity to go to college? His brother, Cody, was jealous, but that didn't count. He was Justin's brother.

Sara had been there too, at the bus stop, to tell Justin good-bye. She had looked at Billy leaning against a light pole across the street, and Justin caught her fleeting smile. To this day, Justin could feel jealous blood pounding in his temples.

Apparently she hadn't noticed, because he felt the familiar touch of her hand on his arm, the brush of her fingertips across his cheek, that prelude to her leaning into him, left foot held high behind her, breasts pressed against his chest, soft lips moving, tongue a teasing reminder of what he'd miss. But they both knew it would end that summer — she'd go back to San Francisco where she belonged. She might visit her grandmother again, but probably not, she had been a college sophomore and the thrill of a two-summer romance with a young cowboy would soon wear off. She'd want to be with her kind.

Now, she probably lived in California. She had written two letters. He still felt guilty about not answering, but he didn't want to think about that now.

Chapter 6

Justin watched William stare out the window as they drove down Cora's wide main street. American flags hung weathered and limp from sidewalk poles, forming a tunnel of red, white and blue through the drab town. He tried to imagine how the place looked to a kid from Manhattan.

"This is where I grew up."

"Thought you grew up on a ranch."

"Yeah, well, this is where I went to school. This is where we shopped, you know what I mean."

"It's weird."

"It's not New York."

Cora reminded him of a patient dying of cancer. Newspapers taped to windows of sad buildings chronicled the town's decline. Weathered plywood smothered the Sears Catalog Store window. He'd fidgeted an eternity away inside that store while his Mom pored over the catalog at things they couldn't afford. She'd called the Sears Catalog her "wish book." She hadn't gotten many wishes.

Four pickups lined the drive-through window at the new State Bank, its red brick walls a contrast to the rest of the town's buildings that had been built from river boulders and sandstone blocks.

They drove past the tallest building in town, a gloomy three-story sandstone box-like structure — the county courthouse.

Parking spaces were full in front of the Cora Café.

"Smells like hamburgers," William said.

"We used to eat there when we came to town. We'll grab a milkshake there later." By then he would have met everyone at the funeral.

"What do you do at a funeral?"

"Not much. Why?"

William shrugged.

"Just stick close to me and I'll show you what to do."

Pickups and cars were scattered across Ludlum's Grocery lot. An elderly couple used a cart as a walker as they pushed their groceries across a cracked blacktop toward their battered car.

At Cora Feed, a man wearing a black cowboy hat backed a three-quarter-ton pickup to a sliding door where a dusty cover-all-clad employee waited with a dolly stacked with fifty-pound sacks of oats. The air carried scents of sweet molasses, oats, salt, corn, dust and hay. Forgotten smells.

"My brother and I used to drive in from the ranch to pick up salt blocks for the cattle."

"Salt blocks?" William asked.

"Big blocks the cows like to lick."

He paused. If he explained salt blocks he would have to explain something else and probably something after that.

Returning to Cora was like something he'd never experienced, and it was hard to put words to those feelings. It was like coming home to a comfortable place, a known place, except for bad memories. But there were good memories too, and like explaining salt blocks, it was more than he wanted to handle.

Two cowboys walked out of Sam's Boots, laughing. The cowboy with a limp carried a plastic bag stretched into a large square.

"That's where my mom bought me my first pair of boots.

How would you like a pair of boots? And a cowboy hat?" he asked.

"Like, not. I don't want to look like a dork," William said.

He drove on down the street and parked across from the Cora Saloon where his parents had spent Saturday nights drinking while he and Cody sat picking on each other, kicking, poking and chasing around the tables. His Mom got drunk one night and screamed something about another woman. She staggered to her feet, grabbed a Coor's bottle and swung at their old man. He ducked. She missed, fell on the table, passed out and then thudded onto the floor. He helped his old man and brother pick her up and drag her toward the door past laughing patrons. At the door, his old man cast a slurred shout at the crowd, "Can't handle whiskey when she's got her period, boys." His old man's words were more embarrassing than her passing out.

The next Monday evening, after receiving a black eye during a school fistfight defending his mother's reputation, he sat at the dinner table praying his Dad wouldn't notice. When he learned Justin had been in a fight, he pushed back from the table. "It's shed time, boy. Gotta teach you from giving our family a reputation as fighters!"

Cody stared at his plate, as always. His mother opened her mouth as if to object, but remained silent when his old man shot her a look. Her fingers worried the napkin and then, as he followed his old man toward the door, she picked up her plate and carried it to the sink. Just as his father opened the door, the plate shattered against the porcelain.

His father spun toward her. "What the hell?"

"I'm sorry . . . it slipped . . . I'm sorry," she said. Justin wondered if she meant she was sorry for the broken plate or sorry for him.

"Don't let it happen again, woman."

Justin shook his head to drive away the memories. His knuckles had turned white gripping the steering wheel. He stretched his fingers and then looked at William.

"What?" the boy asked.

He looked at his watch. He didn't want to arrive at the funeral much before the service.

"I'll show you where I went to school."

He drove around the corner. The school building was tired. Kids played at recess where he'd fooled around with Billy Baxter, Cody and the other kids. A rusted chain-link fence prevented children from running onto the street. That fence, put up new when he'd been in school, had made him feel trapped inside a cage. On the other side of the playground, a barbed-wire fence separated the playground from a cattle pasture. Those had been mostly good days. Better than nights at the ranch.

He parked next to the pasture. A cow raised her tail.

"Jeez, you played right next to cow shit?" William asked.

"Cow pies. They call them cow pies because they're handy," Justin said.

"Useful?"

"When the pioneers crossed the plains, the kids were sent out to collect dried buffalo pies. They used them for cooking fires."

"That's gross!"

He looked at his watch. "Comb your hair. It's time for the funeral."

He drove toward the church and he wondered how he would react if Sara was at the funeral.

Chapter 7

Cars and pickups overflowed the church parking lot. Near the door, people thronged around a tall man wearing a new Stetson — Justin's brother, Cody. He realized, too late, that he should have called Cody to tell him he'd attend the funeral, but then Cody might have insisted they stay at the ranch and he didn't want to get trapped into anything like that.

Time to run the gauntlet, he told himself as he touched his river stone. He found a parking space two blocks away. By the time they walked to the church, most people were inside — all except Cody, a chunky woman standing next to him, and several cowboys.

Cody was a block-like man wearing a tan cowboy shirt and starched jeans over a pair of worn boots. Crinkle lines lined wide-set brown eyes and a weathered face framed a poorly healed broken nose. A stranger would think Cody looked like an honest man, a man who could be a good friend — someone who would be there for you in time of need. But Justin saw him as a man not to be crossed.

Cody spotted them walking up the sidewalk. When they were close, he looked at William, spit a stream of brown tobacco juice into a plastic bottle and then looked back at Justin, "So you came after all."

"Sorry I didn't let you know."

"Our attorney told me. Wasn't a surprise. Figured you'd come back to the smell of money."

"Good to see you, too," Justin said. He offered to shake Cody's hand.

Cody ignored him. "This is my better half, Linda."

The woman's face, framed by curly brown hair, exuded a look of kindness. A crooked eyetooth made her smile comical. She nodded and said she was sorry about their old man's death and then she looked at the boy.

"My son, William."

"Shake your uncle's hand," Cody said.

The wide-eyed boy started to shake hands, but jerked his hand away.

"Gross! Where's your thumb?"

Cody raised his hand for them to see. The knuckle was gone and all that remained was an ugly stump protruding from the meat of his palm. A thin scar of pallid skin covered the end of the bone. "Bad dally," Cody said.

"Huh?"

"I was roping a steer. Threw my loop over the head of this big sucker — nine-hundred-fifty pounds — and I forgot to keep my thumb up when I dallied — that's where you wrap the rope around the saddle horn."

William's eyes became unfocused as if watching a video.

"The rope wrapped my thumb tight to the saddle horn. My horse slid to a stop and when that steer hit the end of the rope, my thumb ripped clean off."

"Insane. Did it hurt?" William asked.

"Hurt like hell. Sometimes the missing part itches. Still miss it, but I learned to live without it," Cody said. He tilted his Stetson back and studied the boy. "Boy, aren't you a chip off the old block!"

"What's that mean?"

"He means you look like me," Justin said.

"Yeah, well, enough small talk. They're waiting for us."

Cody led them into the foyer and nodded to the funeral director who motioned for Justin and William to wait. The man led Cody and Linda down the center aisle to a seat in the reserved front row, and then he returned for Justin and William. He ushered them to the second row and had to wait while people slid over to make room. Justin felt a drop of perspiration slide down from his armpit. He let William into the pew and then he sat behind his brother. If he didn't let investment brokers see him sweat, he wasn't going to reveal his emotions to a church full of hicks.

The pastor conducted a service that was much more personal than those Justin had attended in Manhattan. At least this preacher had known their father. Justin looked at the back of his brother's crew cut head with its hat-tan-line. Cody spit tobacco juice into the bottle. Justin smelled the scent. In eighth grade, Cody had dared him to try chew. Justin took a wad, stuck it in between his cheek and gums, like he'd seen others do, and then he chewed the bitter stuff. His saliva mixed with the tobacco. He tried to spit it out, but swallowed some juice, gagged and vomited. That was his first and last time he tried the disgusting habit.

The service went downhill when the pastor asked if anyone in the audience wanted to share memories about the departed. Justin stuffed down an impulse to share what his old man had done to him, but that would have been totally stupid. No one wanted to hear the truth, particularly at a funeral and particularly if it was ugly. The biggest lies spread about virtues of the "dearly" departed were told at funerals.

A middle-aged woman waddled to the front of the church. She cleared her throat.

"Mr. Thatcher was a wonderful man. When my boy came down with the cancer, him and the sheriff held a fund-raiser to help pay for the treatments. He wasn't in any position to do so, but he donated a steer from his own herd and then he drove around the county and got other ranchers to do the same."

Tears streamed down the woman's face. She attempted to say more, but her voice broke. She began to cry and then she stumbled back toward her seat through a congregation staring at their laps.

Justin looked around, expecting someone to contradict that image of his old man. The most he remembered about his old man's social interactions was at the Cora Saloon, drunk. Instead an endless stream of people came forward and told stories about the goodness of his father. He felt that he'd stumbled into the wrong funeral. They couldn't be talking about *his* old man. Perhaps they'd witnessed his old man's late-in-life facade. Nothing could atone for what he'd done. Nothing.

After the service, mourners jammed into a meeting hall that held faint scents of boiled coffee, cinnamon rolls, aftershave, tobacco, perfume and body sweat, mingled with the barely perceptible odor of disinfectant the janitor had used to mop the tile floors. The Ladies Auxiliary provided coffee, tea, pop, and home-baked cookies, cakes and pies with flaky crusts. William, playing his video game, wandered away through the crowd to find a quiet spot.

Justin stood in a corner, sipping luke-warm coffee from a paper cup while he watched Cody in the center of the room, once again wearing his Stetson, towering over well wishers, chewing tobacco and spitting the juice into the plastic bottle. Cody was the big one, the back slapper, happy-go-lucky, short on intelligence — Justin's polar opposite. They'd once been brothers and best friends, but long droughts wither friendships. They were still brothers, related by their parents' DNA, but Justin wondered how two brothers could be so different.

Old acquaintances drifted up, introduced themselves, offered up memories from school days and then, when conversation stalled, they fidgeted and then struggled for an excuse to drift away.

He watched his old buddy Billy Baxter approach. Justin gave him their old friendship sign. Baxter didn't respond.

"I see you're the sheriff now," Justin said.

"Yep, and the coach of our Little League baseball team."

"Been winning, I noticed."

"You're a little late in coming back, aren't you?" the sheriff said.

Heat rushed to Justin's face, but he remained silent.

The sheriff studied him. "Staying long?"

"No, I have to get back. Business."

"Figured. Have a nice trip." The sheriff turned and walked away.

Justin watched him shake hands and laugh with another man. Several times people approached Justin and said, "Bet you don't remember my name, do you?"

That tactic irritated the hell out of him, so he agreed, "No, I have no idea who you are." Most seemed pleased to score a victory over the dude from Manhattan.

He was listening to a woman he didn't remember tell him that she'd had a high school crush on him when he spotted a stunning woman across the crowded room. She wore a silver belly Stetson and a doeskin vest over a white shirt. She disappeared behind two couples. It could not have been Sara, not after all these years. He realized the woman standing with him had asked him a question. He apologized and asked her to repeat it.

At last one of the couples moved so he could see her once more. He was certain it was Sara. Her sharp teen-age angles had smoothed into a softer sensuality. She was more beautiful than when they'd parted.

Sara visited with people with what was obviously a casual grace grown from friendship. She had the same brilliant smile, the same tilt of the head, the same infectious laughter. She had that familiar habit of touching a person's arm when she said goodbye.

His stomach fluttered, evoking a feeling he'd long ago written off as the response to one's first lover — nothing more.

Her letters had arrived soon after his classes began at Harvard. The first letter had been a happy inquiry. She wanted to know what was happening in his life. She missed him. She asked him to write. He didn't. She wrote again. He sensed a different tone, but he wrote that off to his guilty imagination. Again she asked him to write. He didn't.

He'd moved on, rejected everything from his past, wanted nothing more to do with those memories, even the good ones. She'd stopped writing.

He'd kept both letters, intending to write later, after he was successful. Demands of college, new job, marriage, child, divorce and the concentration required by deal after deal, trumped his good intentions. Maybe there was more to it. He wasn't sure. The years passed and he had never answered. Now, he stood across a crowded room from her, torn between conflicting desires to approach her or flee.

She talked with an elderly couple. They laughed. Her head turned toward him and her smile faded. She looked at him as if she was looking at some cold object. And then she turned back, touched the old man on the arm, said something and then moved away.

Justin wove through the crowd toward her. Cody stopped him to introduce him to a classmate who reminisced about their school days — nothing he wanted to remember. Trapped, he watched Sara moving toward the door.

Justin excused himself and started toward her again, but a couple stopped him to introduce themselves. When he looked again, she had disappeared. He hurried through the crowd to a frosted window still covered by paper snowflakes, someone's idea of a winter wonderland scene. He saw her indistinct form standing next to a truck talking with a tall thin man who looked younger, but Justin couldn't be certain.

They stood close the way secret lovers stand. Justin squeezed his river stone as he watched Sara's hand rise toward the man's face in a slow fluid motion. Her fingertips caressed his cheek and her left foot rose behind her as she leaned into him the same way that she'd said goodbye so many years ago at the bus stop.

Blood pounded and he rubbed his temples. He watched the man climb into the truck and drive away. Sara walked to a red pickup. She drove away from the curb and then, following the other truck, turned at the street corner and disappeared. Justin stared through the glass until the cars and trucks and trees and houses became unfocused.

She was the last person he'd expected to see in Cora. Didn't matter. He'd be flying back to Manhattan tonight and he'd never return. He'd never see her again, just like the woman last night in the bedroom with the neon lights. Maybe that was better. He felt relief, because he didn't know how he'd handle confronting her or how she'd react. He couldn't imagine a scene with a happy ending.

Chapter 8

He turned from the window and walked through the mourners until he found William sitting at a corner table playing his computer game. Justin told him it was time to go.

"Where?"

"I need to see someone before we leave this place."

On the drive to the teacher's house, William asked him what the word "hypocrite" meant.

"Why?"

"I heard some people talking about you."

"How did they use the word?"

"Something like, 'the hypocrite wouldn't come back when his old man was alive.'"

"It means two-faced or insincere."

They parked in front of a one-story home, built during Cora's growth years in the late eighteen hundreds. White stucco smothered the original logs, the roof's hand-split shakes replaced by gray asphalt shingles. The house looked smaller than he remembered.

"I want you to meet the woman who helped me get out of here," Justin said.

"I'll chill out here."

"She'd like to meet you."

"It'll be a yuckfest."

"Miss Adams can tell you some stories you can use later to blackmail me."

William grinned, opened his door and got out.

They walked through blooming lilac bushes that lined the crumbling brick sidewalk toward the porch. The scent reminded him of warm spring days, when she would wear a peasant blouse. She'd bend over his desk to return a paper and he'd smell the lilac fragrance of her perfume. He'd steal a glance at the swell of her wonderful breasts. Her brown eyes sparkled when she spoke to him and her enthusiasm drew him to her like a warm fire on a cold day. She was shorter than his mother, with a small waist and tempting hips. He must have been about William's age when he began fantasizing about her. Even now, he felt guilty, even though he suspected he wasn't the only boy in the class who'd thought of her that way.

He rang her doorbell and wondered what to expect. They waited. He rang again. Nothing. Giving up, they turned back toward the car. Halfway down the sidewalk, they heard the door creak open. They looked back.

A blue-veined hand clung to the doorframe. The woman's other hand clawed around the handle of a cane. She had a wrinkled face, framed by permed gray hair and old-fashioned glasses.

He now knew what a dying person looked like. He shuddered. William's hand sought his, which gave him unexpected comfort. He squeezed the boy's hand and they walked back to the porch.

She wore a dark dress and black shoes. Pain dulled eyes stared through the opaque film of cataracts.

"Yes?"

"Miss Adams? I'm Justin Thatcher. This is my son, William."

"Justin! You came back after all. And you brought your son. Oh! I never expected to meet my William. How wonderful!

Wonderful! Come in."

He recognized her voice, even though age had roughened its tone. Her former enthusiasm now seemed like dying embers, yet her voice carried hints of joy from the past. Time and disease made her body unrecognizable. He kissed her shrunken cheek and smelled an old woman.

She shuffled toward the living room, cane tapping a path on a hardwood floor. Slivers of light knifed through gaps of drawn curtains. Dust particles floated through an odor of dead flowers.

William's nostrils flared. The boy's hand squeezed tighter. He squeezed back, as much to give himself assurance as to his son. He also felt protective. That was a new experience.

She folded herself into a chair, sighed and motioned them to a couch. William stared at crocheted arm doilies, sat down and crossed his arms over his stomach. Justin remembered the room being larger when he and Cody had studied at the corner table.

"How was the funeral?" she asked.

"Just fine," Justin said.

"Your Daddy was a better man than you think."

"Really?" Justin asked.

"I hope you'll change your mind. Maybe later."

Grimacing, she reached for the table lamp, arthritic fingers twisting the switch until the light came on. Light flooded a picture of her as a young woman, smiling, the way he remembered, her breasts shadowed by the photographer's cowboy hat.

"Your daddy was such a good boy, William," she said. "He was different than the others. He had dreams. He was my very best student. Most students think only about today. Your daddy thought about the future and wanted his to be big. He's done it, too. I'm so proud of him."

"Miss Adams was my teacher all through grade school. My brother and I stayed here when storms closed the mountain pass between town and the ranch. We studied at that table."

"Your daddy also had a little devil in him," she said.

"Not now, Miss Adams."

"Oh, it won't hurt William to know about the time you put the cow in the new principal's office."

A slow grin crossed William's face.

"The principal was officious and he deserved it," she said.

"It was Billy Baxter's idea," Justin said.

"Sure." William said.

"You're right William, Billy Baxter didn't have enough brains to think up something like that. Still doesn't, but he did get elected sheriff."

"What did the SWAT team do?" William asked.

"SWAT? What?"

"Let's talk about something . . . "

"Oh hush, Justin. William should know his daddy wasn't perfect. That cow made a mess by the time the principal opened his office on Monday morning. Wet cow pies everywhere. He went crazy and made your daddy clean up before he suspended him."

William pushed the hair from his eyes, "Suspended?"

Justin ignored the tight little Ashley-smile.

"Not for long. I persuaded the school board to pressure the principal to drop the suspension," Miss Adams said.

William gave him a hard look. "Like it must have been nice to have someone stick up for you."

"Only fair," Miss Adams continued. "Someone tattled and the principal accused your daddy. He confessed, but he protected Billy and Cody. He took the blame."

"You didn't rat out on them?"

"No, I didn't," Justin said. The boy was going to chew on this like a dog with a bone.

"Uh-huh."

"I also keep my promises. After Miss Adams helped me get the scholarship to college, I told her that if I ever had the money,

I'd start a scholarship in her name." He took the scholarship program documents from his briefcase and handed the papers to her.

While she read, he counted twelve different colored pills scattered on the table.

"Too much. Too much." She dropped the papers and her glasses in her lap.

She pulled a lace handkerchief from her sleeve and dabbed her eyes. "You've been so good to me. Did you know William, your Daddy made it possible for me to stay in my home? He sent a check every month. He kept me out of the nursing home." She turned to Justin. "I don't know how to thank you."

Justin remembered she took three months before she cashed the first check — necessity trumped dignity. Her breath made a whizzing sound.

"Are you all right, Ellen?"

"The excitement wore me out. You need to go. I'm sorry, but I'm too tired to walk you to the door. I hope you don't mind."

"You need to sign the scholarship documents." Justin reached for his pen.

"I want to read them carefully. You'll have to come back."

Justin shook his head. This was like the first check he had sent her, all over again. Why couldn't she just accept his gratitude?

"The doctor will be here tomorrow," she continued. "After that, I'll be too tired to talk. Come day after tomorrow at ten o'clock. I'll leave the front door unlocked."

"We're flying back this afternoon," he said.

"There are no late afternoon flights."

"We're on a private jet."

"Then you can do whatever you want, including fly back the day after tomorrow."

That was the Miss Adams he remembered. He'd never been able to say no to the woman, but he didn't want to go back to his old man's place. Didn't want to dredge up memories. Didn't want the damned nightmares. Didn't want Cody's presence to remind him that Justin had left him behind, alone. But William wanted to see the ranch. And before he knew it, he'd made a promise to Miss Adams that he'd see her the day after tomorrow.

Chapter 9

They drove away from Miss Adam's house in silence for several minutes before William spoke.

"You were suspended, too."

"It's not the same."

"Cow shit is worse than a confetti bomb."

"Nobody called the SWAT team," Justin said.

"Would if they could have."

"Maybe."

"I'm just like you." The boy glanced at him, looking for a reaction and when there was none, he looked out the passenger side window.

The attorney's office was in a small house on Tenth Street. A front yard sign, painted with neat black letters, announced: Ed Highstreet – Lawyer. The cramped reception area smelled like mold. The secretary told them Highstreet was on the phone and would be with them shortly.

In the reception waiting area, the wooden chairs creaked. Thumbed magazines littered a table: *Outdoor Life, Stockman's Journal* and *Horse & Rider*.

Several minutes later, the lawyer greeted them. He was a thin man in his early seventies. Glasses with black rims and thick lenses magnified his eyes. Justin had heard about the family, long-time Cora residents, mostly cattle ranchers. Highstreet was the first to get a college degree and he'd returned to Cora to set up a law practice about the time Justin left for Harvard.

"Why don't you join us, William?" Justin asked.

"I'm cool." He had gone back to his game.

"Might learn something."

"I'm about to break into a new level."

Justin hid his irritation behind a smile. He thought he'd been making progress pulling the kid out of his digital world. He'd been wrong.

Inside, the lawyer's desk was stacked high with documents. As soon as Justin sat in a wooden armchair in front of the desk, Highstreet opened a file and read to himself. Justin watched the man's lips move. Several minutes later, the door behind him groaned open and shut. He turned and looked up at his brother. Arms crossed, Cody leaned against the door and studied him as if he were a bull at a stockyard auction.

"Time's done you well, Justin. Not as scraggly as when you pulled out of here — put on some weight, got yourself a fancy haircut, fancy clothes. Smell a whole lot better than when I drove you to the bus. Remember that? What's it been? Twenty-eight years?"

Justin rose to face his brother.

"Sorry about the way we started back there outside the church," Cody continued. "I was nervous. No hard feelings?" He offered his right hand. His left hand clutched the bottle half-filled with tobacco spit.

Justin gripped his brother's massive, callused hand that sprouted a rough knob instead of a thumb. Then Cody stepped over a chair like swinging into a saddle. He raised his Stetson and rubbed his crew cut with the stub of his thumb and then he settled the hat, tugging down on the brim.

"Told Ed you needed to know which way the wind was blowing. It's bad. We're between a rock and a hard place."

The lawyer picked up a page from the file. "Well . . ."

Cody cut him off. "Don't hold nothing back."

"Give me a chance, Cody."

"Sorry. Just don't want us to waste time on small stuff when the big stuff is in play. Right, Justin?"

He ignored Cody.

The lawyer studied a sheet of paper. "The two of you are the joint beneficiaries of the estate that includes the ranch, water and mineral rights, livestock and equipment."

"The will makes Justin executor. That means he has sole power to make decisions. He can buy, sell or negotiate on behalf the estate."

Justin felt his pulse quicken like at the beginning of a business deal. "What's its value?"

The lawyer looked up at Justin. "Cattle prices fell and ranch lost money. Farm Credit had the mortgage and to keep up with the payments, your father took out a personal loan from the Cora State Bank. He then borrowed more money from the Production Credit Association for a registered herd. They usually bring more money. Prices tanked again and your father could not make the payments. When that loan defaulted, the cattle were sold at a loss and then the sheriff, at a public bankruptcy auction, sold a certificate of mortgage to the Cora State Bank.

"State law gives former owners the right to repurchase their property out of bankruptcy until the end of the redemption period. Your deadline is May thirtieth."

"Two weeks to buy back a ranch that's leveraged to the hilt?" Justin asked.

"That's an inheritance for you," Cody said through his teeth.

"You can buy it back any time during the next two weeks, but the loans, back taxes, penalties and interest are more than its market value as a working ranch," the attorney said.

"Who bought the mortgage?" Justin asked.

"Kurt Kamm, the banker, bought a certificate of purchase," the attorney said.

Justin was silent for a moment. He remembered seeing ads for ranches offering fishing and hunting in the *Wall Street Journal.*

"You said 'working ranch.' Does it have a higher value as a recreation property?"

Cody leaned forward. "Haven't been any sales around here, but elsewhere places like ours have gotten pretty valuable to rich outsiders like you."

Justin resented the remark, but Cody was right; locals now considered him a rich outsider, just like everyone else from Manhattan who'd bought property out West.

"So what would it sell for?" Justin asked.

"Your place might be attractive because it's deeded from the river bottom hay fields all the way up to the top of Coulter Mountain," Highstreet said.

"It won't do any good to find a buyer," Cody said.

"Why not?"

"I'll never leave the ranch. Was born there, was raised there, live there, and that's where I'm going to die."

"Look Cody, a smart businessman explores every alternative to maximize value of an asset," Justin said.

"Wall Street bullshit," Cody said.

Justin turned to Highstreet. "What would be the value of our ranch to the right buyer?"

"Someplace north of six and south of ten."

Justin never imagined the ranch might be worth real money. Obviously this was not a deal he was going to let slip through his fingers. Cody could buy a smaller, more productive place with his share of the money. So what if it wasn't near Cora, Montana.

Cody slapped his hat on a knee. "Goddamnit! Told you I'd never sell."

"You don't have a lot of choice, unless Justin wants to buy the ranch," Highstreet said.

Cody looked at Justin. "Well?"

"I don't have that kind of money."

"That's more bullshit. You're rich," Cody said.

"I have no liquidity — everything I own is equity that's locked up in the business." And that was today's truth. Tomorrow, after he returned to Manhattan, paid off Farnsworth's loan and liquidated his equity position he would be flush, but he wasn't about to invest in that god-forsaken place that wouldn't produce a return on his investment.

Cody jammed the Stetson low over his eyes.

Justin listened to Cody's wheezing and looked at a picture on the wall. It was an old print of two cowboys in yellow slickers on horseback herding cattle — a dying way of life. He turned back to the attorney. "How long would it take to find a buyer at those prices?"

"A year or two at least. You can't sell your ranch before the end of the redemption period. Maybe, if you had an appraisal worth ten million, you could get someone to give you a bridge loan, but they'd need to be assured that you'll meet the payments until it's sold."

"Could the local banker swing a deal that big?" Justin asked.

"Do you know Kurt Kamm?" the attorney asked.

"I don't remember him. Did he go to school with us?" Justin asked Cody.

"Ten years ahead of us. He's a fourth generation Montanan and real proud of it. His grandpa homesteaded a place about seventy miles east of town. Kurt brags his kin shot the last of the Indians around here. Claims to have the scalps, but I've never seen them. He's got a face like a bulldog chewing a wasp, but he's a good guy."

Justin smiled. "A good guy?"

"Volunteers and does a lot of good, like when the county couldn't afford it, Kurt bought two new trucks — one for the sheriff and one for Search and Rescue. He's a volunteer deputy. Helps out when Billy's out of town coaching our Little League team. Without our asking, Kurt came out to help with the calving last spring after a snowstorm. Knew we couldn't do it alone. We pulled thirty together," Cody said.

Highstreet coughed into his fist. "Kurt also has a reputation of doing anything for a profit."

"Yeah, there are a lot of stories about him using his power. But there are stories about everyone," Cody said.

"Maybe he'll have an idea. I'll meet with him," Justin said.

They walked out of Highstreet's office to the reception area where they met William.

"You ride as good as your Dad?" Cody asked.

"Ride?" William said.

"He means horses," Justin added.

"I don't know. Dad's never taken me riding."

Cody studied the boy for a few seconds. "Well, you can learn."

"We're staying in Missoula," Justin said.

"Can't get this close without coming home," Cody said.

Justin's jaw tensed. "I need to visit the banker."

"Suit yourself." Then Cody nodded toward William. "I've got to run a couple errands. Bill could . . ."

Justin cut him off. "It's William."

"Yeah . . . like I was saying, William could have a milk-shake at the café while you meet with Kurt. Meet us later there. Linda wants to visit with you."

"Do they have good hamburgers?" William asked.

"The best damned burgers in the world! I'll buy as many as you can eat, if you'd teach me how to play that thing," Cody pointed to the game player.

"Wicked!" William said.

"Huh?" Cody asked.

"He means that's okay. It's kid slang," Justin said.

"Not around here, it isn't. We talk American. Let's go over to the café," Cody said.

"Is Kamm married to anyone I should remember?" Justin asked.

"Beverly Johnstone. She's just as wild as ever. Proves you can lead a whore to culture, but you can't make her think." Cody laughed.

Justin gave him a not-in-front-of-William look.

The boy didn't even try to hide his grin.

Chapter 10

A few minutes later, Justin walked into the Cora State Bank and gave the receptionist his name. She told him she was sorry about his father and then asked him to wait while she informed the president. She walked toward a glass-walled office, where Kamm sat, alligator boots propped on his desk, reading the weekly *Chronicle*.

Kamm looked over the top of the paper at her and then glanced at him. Justin smiled. Cody had been right, the pudgy bald man's face looked like he'd just swallowed a wasp. The banker quickly folded the paper, placed it on his desk and then hurried out to greet Justin.

"It's wonderful to meet you in person, Mr. Thatcher. I've heard so much about you from your father. Thank you for stopping."

He emanated a scent of cheap aftershave. Kamm's fat lips formed an obsequious smile, yet the pupils of his black eyes were tiny pinpoints, as if he had something to hide. His head bobbed up and down over a weak handshake. He guided Justin into his office, offered him a chair and then scurried around the desk and sat down.

"I understand you bought the certificate to our ranch mortgage at the bankruptcy auction," Justin said.

"I feel real bad about that. Your father needed money and so

I made your old man a personal loan. Then cattle prices tanked and forced your father into bankruptcy. I already had a lien on the property. Had to cover my ass by purchasing the foreclosure deed. Now I own it."

"Not yet." Justin said. "We're still within the redemption period."

"Thank goodness! Now all you have to do is go down to the courthouse and write out a check. I'm relieved! I didn't know how I'd ever get my money back."

"Plus your profit."

Kamm averted his eyes and shifted in his chair as though he had a cramp in his back.

"Yes. Of course, plus my interest, but I don't look at that as profit. I . . ." He was interrupted by a voice from a radio on his credenza. He reached over and turned down the volume.

"I'm sorry for the interruption, Mr. Thatcher. I'm the volunteer driver for our Search and Rescue truck, so I have to listen to the sheriff's dispatcher in case I'm needed."

"Of course, Mr. Kamm. As you were saying?"

"There's no profit on the deal. Back taxes, penalties, interest and loans are above its market value. You can't sell it for a profit. Your family has never made a decent return off it. So, unless you want a play thing, and if you're looking at it as a businessman, how do you expect to make a return on your money?"

"Some things are worth more than money," Justin lied.

Kamm leaned forward and propped his elbows on the desk.

"I could come out even on the deal, but it's going to take a long time."

"Perhaps you have an idea that would help both of us."

"I can't think of anything, not unless you want to buy it. But it would be a lousy investment. Probably better that you and your brother forget it."

Justin stared at the man. He was sending mixed signals.

"If you knew our family could never make money from the

ranch, why did you make him the loan?"

The banker eyes widened. "Look, I felt sorry for your old man. He helped a lot of people around here in little ways. He and Sheriff Baxter held a couple fundraisers to help out people in trouble, but you know that — you heard how he helped that boy with cancer. There were others. We're a small community. We have to help each other. That's why I loaned him the money. Knew better, but that's my mistake. I'm stuck with it and I take responsibility for my mistakes."

Justin walked out of the bank and past the Search and Rescue truck in the parking lot. He was troubled by the conversation. In his car, he used his cell phone to call his investigator. He ordered him to check if there were any known oil or gas reserves or exploration in the area. For good measure, he asked him to look into Kurt Kamm.

"The banker is covering up something and I want to know what. Dig deep."

Chapter 11

Justin walked into the Cora Café, enveloped by the aroma of baking bread. He'd stepped into a time warp. The same photos of the 1950's football teams adorned the walls. The café owner had played on that team. Signatures had been scrawled over every surface, tables, walls and ceiling, to immortalize generations of high school seniors. He spotted his name, and Cody's, and Billy Baxter's, but not Sara's. She'd been an outsider, a big city girl who visited her grandparents' ranch during school vacations. Her grandparents were outsiders as well; they went south every winter. Locals called them "summer people."

Men and women, dressed in funeral attire, sat at Formica-topped tables. Faces turned toward him. Conversations dropped to a low buzz. Wooden booths with seventy years worth of carved initials lined the north and east walls. People sat on stools at the lunch counter that guarded a waitress workspace. There were six Hamilton Beach shake machines and a glass pie case bracketing the kitchen pass-through.

Linda waved from a back booth. William sat next to his uncle, sporting a new cowboy hat.

Justin threaded his way through tables toward the booth, avoiding curious eyes. One man smiled. He returned the smile. Several others nodded at him. He nodded back. This was like walking into school after one of his old man's weekend drunks.

Cody motioned him into the booth.

There was a sparkle in William's eyes as he touched his hat. "Uncle Cody bought it for me. How do you like it?"

"You look like a dork," Justin said.

William replied with a dismissive grunt.

Cody laughed. "Told him he was going go blind trying to see through that hair. Suggested the barber, but he's as stubborn as his old man."

"You know Justin, you might want to buy some work clothes before we drive back to the ranch," Linda said.

"We're staying in Missoula. My khakis are just fine," Justin said.

"There you go." Cody turned to William. "See what I mean about being stubborn? So, did Kurt have an idea for us to save the ranch?"

"He seemed a bit passive-aggressive," Justin said.

"That's too bad. He gets in bad moods sometimes. In fact, he can get downright mean if he doesn't get his way. Maybe he'll change his mind and come up with an idea," Cody said.

A plump waitress, in her late sixties, sporting her high school hairstyle, approached the table.

"Betty, this is my brother, Justin."

"I'm sorry about your father, Mr. Thatcher. He was a wonderful man. He told me so many nice things about you."

Justin stared at her. He couldn't imagine his old man would have said anything about him, let alone anything "nice." He remembered the countless times he had sat silent, wanting to vanish, while his Dad bragged to anyone who'd listen about Cody's exploits.

William ordered a cheeseburger, fries and chocolate shake. The waitress took the rest of their orders and left.

"Cat got your tongue, Justin?" Cody asked.

"I was surprised Dad said anything about me."

"That was our old man for you. Never said nothing nice to

your face, always talked nice about you behind your back."

Justin shook his head. Even though he remembered some of the details from their sporadic Christmas cards, he turned to Linda and asked her to tell him about herself.

"I'm the daughter of a Forest Service ranger who moved into the district several years after you left. My parents retired and live down in Arizona. We have two grown daughters living in Seattle." She glanced at William. "Cody and I always wanted a son. But after our second daughter, the doctor said I couldn't have any more children."

"I'm sorry," Justin said.

The burgers, shakes, French fries and coffee arrived. Linda asked William about school. Between gulps, he talked about Collegiate.

"I was suspended . . . just like Dad was."

Linda and Cody looked at Justin. He changed the subject, telling them about his life, but it was clear their attention was an act of politeness and not interest.

Cody grabbed his fork and stabbed several fries, dunked them in a pool of ketchup and then shoveled them into his mouth. A spot of ketchup stained his chin.

"Do you have a lot of horses at the ranch, Uncle Cody?"

"Not as many as we used to. One stallion, eleven geldings, two mares and two foals."

Linda leaned over and wiped the ketchup off Cody's chin. He smiled at her.

"What are geldings?" William asked.

"Cut stallions," Cody said.

"Yeah?"

"Geldings are stallions that have been castrated," Justin said.

"Yuck!"

"Maybe 'yuck,' but good business, William. First, you only need one stud to service the mares. Second, castrating them calms them down, makes them easier to work," Cody said.

"What's a foal?" William asked.

"A baby horse that hasn't been weaned," Cody said.

"Sure, I knew that."

Linda smiled, "We had two foals last month, Billy."

"They call him William," Cody said.

"Oh."

"Family name from his mother's side," Justin said. Ashley and her father had been insistent about the formal first name. He'd decided not to start a war over something inconsequential. Maybe he'd been wrong.

"Well, those foals are the cutest things you've ever seen, William. We'll show them to you this evening. They need attention. You can pet them," Linda said

He looked at his dad. "We are going, aren't we?"

He knew when he'd lost. In business that was as important as knowing when he'd won.

"It's a long way back to Missoula."

"We built our own cabin since you left, so you can stay in your old place. Cleaned it yesterday. You'll enjoy showing William where you grew up," Linda said.

Justin was trapped.

Chapter 12

Linda suggested that Cody, Justin and William drive the pickup to the ranch, while she drove the rental car with the groceries. "It'll be good for you boys to be together for a spell."

Justin sat in the middle of the front bench seat so William could better see the view out the side window. Twenty minutes later, Cody turned off the blacktop onto a dirt road that zigzagged up the shoulder of a mountain. He drove well with his crippled hand.

William spotted a herd of deer feeding on the spring grass of a west-facing slope. Justin explained why they were called "mule" deer: their ears are huge and they run with stiff-legged bounces.

Justin hadn't thought about deer for a long time. He had shot a buck when he was twelve, the autumn after his Mom disappeared. It was dark by the time he gutted the buck. A thick fog had obscured the mountains. Trying to return to the ranch, he became lost and spent the night curled under a rock ledge, alone and frightened. Shivering in the dark, listening for the footsteps of a hungry grizzly, he swore he would learn everything about survival. And, during the next several years, he checked out and devoured every book from the library about Indian and outdoorsman's skills.

After the fog lifted the next morning, thrilled with his first kill, he ran back to the ranch, breathless and certain his dad would be proud. His dad acted as if he had not noticed Justin had been missing. Later, Cody told him their old man had been worried, but Justin didn't know if he'd said that just to make him feel better.

They saddled a horse to pack out the carcass. When his old man saw the deer, he said, "Only a two-point, for Christ sake. Next time kill a big one."

Several miles later, William pointed out another deer herd. The boy's eyes glinted with an excitement Justin had never before witnessed. The kid was fun to be around at a time like this.

Cody continued driving up through the switchbacks. He stopped at a small white cross that had been planted on the narrow shoulder.

"Here's where Dad died," Cody said.

They got out to look. Cody had painted "Richard Thatcher" in neat black letters on the cross-arm. Red and yellow plastic flowers had been wired to the marker. Justin remembered all the sullen times his old man had driven them to and from school and what a relief it had been when Justin could drive.

William looked over the cliff. "How far did he fall?"

"Almost a thousand feet. Had to call in a helicopter to haul him out. Truck's still down there," Cody said.

Justin looked at the cross and then stepped to the edge of the cliff, peered over and felt nothing but a cold updraft that made his eyes water.

"Think he had a heart attack?" Justin asked.

"Nope. Something was fishy about his accident. When I got here there were other tracks that looked spun-out like when you're pushing someone and spin your tires."

"What did the sheriff say?" Justin asked.

"That it was my imagination," Cody said.

"You were always big on conspiracy theories," Justin said as he climbed back into the truck.

At the crest of the pass, Cody pulled onto a turn off and set the brake and turned to William. "They call this Dead Man's Pass. Can you guess why?"

"Someone died up here?" William asked.

"Back in the early days, a late spring blizzard killed a fur trapper right here. People can get fooled about weather in this country. Still happens. Just a few years ago, it was real warm in May, just like this year, and a spring storm rolled in and dumped four feet of wet snow on the high country. Three cowboys and their horses froze to death," Cody said

"Gross," William said.

They stepped out to look down at a green valley that narrowed in the distance toward snow-topped peaks. A river twisted like a blue ribbon through the forest. The sky held a sharp clarity. Justin inhaled the fresh air and tried to force his body to relax, but his muscles were tense with foreboding of how he would react when he arrived at the ranch.

Cody walked to the edge of the cliff, unzipped his pants and turned away. Justin joined him.

"You might want to go, William, it's still a long drive," Justin said.

"Here?" The boy glanced up and down the road.

Cody laughed. "Ever pee outside in New York City?"

"Sure, lots of times," William lied as he stepped between them and struggled with his zipper.

"Never want to piss into the wind . . . you'll wet yourself," Cody said.

"I know that!" William said, in the same tone of voice.

Cody nodded at Justin. "Just look at that boy's stream. Oh, to be young again!"

William stood taller.

"Can you smell the pine trees, William?" Justin asked.
"Cool."

High on the mountain slopes, lodge pole pine mixed with

giant Douglas fir. On the right side of the valley, black volcanic mountains formed an impenetrable barrier. The left side rounded into tree-ringed meadows.

"This place is wicked," William said.

"It isn't wicked," Cody said, voice tinged with anger.

"He means it's wonderful," Justin said.

"Well damnit, teach your kid to speak American."

Justin had looked at this valley thousands of times as a boy and it hadn't seemed impressive. He'd taken it for granted. Now, seeing it as though for the first time through his son's eyes, the land looked different. It wasn't as he'd imagined.

He put an arm around his son's shoulders. William hugged his waist. It was the first time the little snot had shown any affection. Justin felt more emotion than he expected.

Cody pointed to the valley. "That's my church, and way up there near the head of the valley is our home place. This is where your Daddy and I was born and grew up."

"What's that, Uncle Cody?" William pointed to an animal silhouetted against the sky on the limestone ridge above them.

"Wolf!" Cody scrambled to the back seat for a pair of binoculars. He handed the glasses to William.

"He has something wrong with one ear. It's got two points — like an M."

Justin took the binoculars. The lone wolf stood broadside forty yards above the road. A gust of wind rippled its back hair. A pink tongue licked lips. The ears flattened as the long muzzle rose toward the sky. The wolf howled a low moan that rose to a wail. The sound reminded Justin of the hollow loneliness he'd felt after his mother disappeared. He'd been eleven, the same age as William was now. He wondered if loneliness would consume William after they returned to Manhattan to experience Ashley's absence.

The wolf's golden-yellow eyes focused on him — not just *on* him, but also *into* him, as if searching his soul. Justin's scalp tingled.

The wolf raised its head and howled once more before it trotted out of sight over the ridge.

"That's a rare sight, William. Wolves usually run in family packs. When a young one matures, he leaves the pack. It's called a lone wolf. This one could be a lone wolf looking for a mate, or the rest of the pack could be just over the ridge," Justin said.

"Are there other wolves here, Uncle Cody?"

"I've seen an occasional track, but don't think there's a pack living here. Our old man, he hated them — shot at every one he spotted. I guess they're okay so long as they don't begin eating livestock and people's dogs and cats. Wolves were here before white men. Like us, they belong. Fun to look at in any event," Cody said.

"That was insane," William said.

Cody gave the boy a hard look but then smiled. "What'd you say?"

"I mean that was . . . great," William grinned.

They got in the truck and drove down the switchbacks toward the valley. Justin looked out the back window, hoping once more to spot the wolf. And he wondered why he would feel a connection.

Chapter 13

Fifteen miles up valley from the bottom of Dead Man's Pass, they drove past Squaw Creek Trail, a horse trail that climbed a ridge into the wilderness. It was the trail he and Sara had ridden to a long-ago picnic, the first time they'd made love. It seemed that day had happened yesterday. He could still recall the smell of her breath, fresh and sweet at their first kiss, deepening as their passion rose until deeper, body-wracking gasps brought up an aroma of something darkly primitive. The remembered scent of her breath aroused him again.

He'd loved her scents. She had always smelled fresh — fresh soap, fresh laundry or fresh sweat. Under those scents were other smells that he'd discovered by sniffing at her throat, between her breasts, down her stomach and between her legs with the fruity aroma that so excited him. No other woman had ever smelled like Sara.

He wondered if that was why he kept trying out women, like he'd tried out the one after the MOMA charity event, testing her scent. If so, she'd failed. They all failed. Ashley included.

On a brighter note, he wondered if his attraction to Sara had been pure animal physicality, or if given time, they could have fallen in love. But now he wasn't sure about love, if it truly existed or it was merely a concept made up by romantics.

Ten minutes later, they drove past the only other ranch in

the valley, once owned by Sara's grandparents. Justin asked, "What happened to Sara Parson?"

"Didn't you talk with her at the funeral?" Cody asked.

"She was across the room. We didn't get to talk."

Cody looked at him. "She married a fellow from Silicone Valley by the name of Frank Sterling. They moved out here with their kid. Frank . . ."

William interrupted him and pointed to a herd of animals grazed in a clearing in the timber. "What are those animals?"

Cody told him they were elk. He pointed out several cow elk that would soon give birth to calves. The elk spotted their truck and trotted stiff legged toward the timber, heads held high to pick up the scent of danger.

Justin thought better about asking anything more about Sara, like what was her relationship with that young guy she'd met after the funeral. Not now, not in front of William. Not when the boy still hurt from Ashley's leaving.

Twenty minutes later, Cody pulled over next to a buck-and-rail fenced pasture that ran from the road to the river. He turned off the engine and pointed to their ranch.

The property ran two miles east and west from the road across pastures, through the cottonwoods along the bank of the freestone river, up through lower mountain benches of meadow and pine to the top of Coulter Mountain. The place looked green and peaceful, yet Justin's stomach soured when he recalled his old man and the shed.

A herd of horses grazed in the pasture. Cody pointed out a short bay named Baily that had been his daughter's horse.

"You can help me gather them into the corrals before breakfast," Cody told William.

"Before breakfast? You gotta be kidding," William said.

"Cowboys do chores first thing. Your Daddy hated morning chores." Cody grinned.

Justin glared at Cody.

"Is that true, Dad?"

Justin ran his hand through his hair. "Things were complicated. Our mother disappeared . . ."

"Like Mom?" William asked.

"We know where your mom is. We could call her in an emergency."

"She left me alone, just like you were left alone."

Cody pulled his Stetson low, crossed his arms and stared out the window.

"It's not the same," Justin said.

The air in the cab had turned sour. Cody rolled down the windows and started the engine. "Yeah. Well, we'd better get moving." They drove through a log gate with a sign hanging from the crossbeam:

Thatcher & Sons Registered Angus Cattle

The truck's tires crunched on the gravel driveway. Baily trotted toward the truck and the other horses followed. The herd broke into a gallop, leaping irrigation ditches, bucking and kicking.

The fragrant scent of pasture grass flooded the cab. Cody stopped. They watched the herd gallop toward them and listened to hoof beats echo against the earth. The herd slid to a stop just short of the truck, showering it with gravel.

A horse stuck his head through the passenger side window. William shrank against his dad, eyes wide with fear.

"Baily wants you to stroke his nose," Cody said.

William raised his hand and then jerked back from munching lips. The horse raised its nose. William scooted into his dad's lap.

"He thinks you have a cube. Reach over his lips and rub his forehead," Justin said.

William raised his hand. Baily's lips chomped. The boy fell backward, his head in Cody's lap.

"Buck up," Cody said.

"Huh?"

"Cody means 'be brave'," Justin said.

He took his son's hand in his, raised it slowly and touched the horse's forehead. Baily responded by lowering his head and sniffing the seat where William had been sitting. Justin withdrew his hand and William petted the horse until it backed away.

"Insane!" William brushed the hair from his eyes, scooted into his own seat, his face split by a grin.

Several minutes later, they drove past the corrals and the barn, where on frigid mornings Justin had balanced on a one-legged stool and milked the cow, his cold fingers squeezing her teats while she slapped the back of his head with the end of her tail, a frozen hammer of hair, urine and shit.

"What's that stink?" William asked.

"Smells great, doesn't it? You can wash horseshit off, but you can't get it out of your blood." Cody cut a glance at Justin.

Justin felt acid surge up into his esophagus as they drove the quarter of a mile from the barn through a strip of pine trees toward the cabins and the shed. He touched his river stone to protect him from the memories.

Chapter 14

The shed leaned down-wind, door sagging from rusted hinges, wooden roof shingles curled upward as if frightened. There were wide cracks between the wind-blasted planks. At night, spiders crawled out. At least they always had, so he assumed they still did. Justin swallowed hard to keep the bitter taste from his throat.

"There's our new place." Cody nodded toward a one-story log cabin that had a red metal roof and double pane glass windows set in metal frames. It was larger than the homestead cabin.

There were lawns and flowerbeds where a few tight-curled flower heads peeked from the earth as if reluctant to be caught by a late snowstorm. There had been no flowers or lawn when he'd left — just mud and horseshit. Helped to have a woman around.

A red heeler rushed the truck, barking.

"That's Otto. He protects the place," Cody said.

Justin pointed out the cabin where they'd grown up. It was smaller than he remembered. Everything seemed smaller. Except the shed.

The original cabin's second story, added for the boys' bedroom, had been made with vertical log slabs. He'd spent hours alone in that bedroom, staring out the window at the empty driveway, praying for his mom to come back. His old man told the sheriff that he'd seen tail lights driving down the driveway the night she disappeared, suggesting their mom had abandoned them for another man. The disappearing tail light story formed such a strong image in Justin's mind that he actually believed he'd watched her driving away from them. Maybe he had.

"You boys unpack and come over to our cabin for supper when you hear the bell," Cody said.

"What bell, Uncle Cody?"

Cody pointed to a large bell mounted on a ten-foot-tall pole next to the rock sidewalk. "Got it off an old locomotive."

"Ding-dong, hoot-toot! That's wicked."

"American," Cody said.

"I'll try."

Justin looked at the boy and remembered his mother's saying, "Every cloud has a silver lining." Maybe Cody could teach the boy some respect.

"Linda will ring the bell fifteen minutes before meal time, so you'll know when to wash up and come over."

"Can I ring it?" William asked.

Cody laughed. "You can be the official bell ringer, starting tomorrow."

They got out of the truck and Otto jumped on William and licked his face.

"He likes you," Cody said.

The dog sniffed Justin's leg and growled. Cody called the dog off and then grinned. "Come over after you get settled."

Justin carried their suitcases and climbed plank stairs to the front porch.

"Snow piles as high as the porch in the winter, William."

"We get snow in New York, you know."

He led the boy into the mudroom, with a wooden bench along the right side, a V-shaped boot puller on the floor, coat and hat pegs in the walls. The left side of the room was devoted to log storage. "This is where I stacked firewood."

They walked through the inner door into a combination living room-kitchen. It was as if he'd left yesterday.

"What's that stink?" William asked.

"Ashes from the woodstove. That's how we heat the cabin."

The smell brought back good memories from before his mom disappeared: doing his homework on the floor in front of the crackling stove, enveloped in aromas of baking bread and venison steaks sizzling in the frying pan, and the sounds of plates and silverware clinking together as his mother set the table. The later memories were different. That's when he'd started spending more time in town with Miss Adams. Doing homework there. Staying there as much as possible.

On the far wall, the steel barrel stove dominated a river rock facade that protected the wood paneling from scorching. A black pipe from the back of the stove ran through an insulating metal collar in the ceiling.

A metal grate in the ceiling above the stove allowed heat and the smell of frying bacon to rise into the upstairs bedroom. On frigid dark winter mornings, he had stood barefoot on the grill, pulling on heavy clothes, jostling Cody away from the warmest spot.

"I don't like that smell," William said.

Justin had forgotten the wood stove scent.

"You'll get used to it. You might even learn to enjoy it."

"Not!"

He looked at the old man's naugahyde La-Z-Boy, a wingbacked chair and a couch with frayed cushions. His mother used to sit in the wing chair close to the lamp, needles clicking a soothing rhythm as she knit sweaters for her boys. His father sat in the La-Z-Boy and drank whiskey. Justin tasted some of his whiskey once. It was terrible stuff, and he couldn't see how anybody could drink it.

William looked around the room. "Boy, that's an old TV set."

"We didn't have TV back then," he told William.

"Why not?"

"Mountains blocked the signals. It was before satellite TV."

"Did you watch DVDs?"

Justin laughed. "I grew up in ancient times. No DVD, no TV, no iPods, no GameBoys and really lousy radio reception."

The boy looked at him as if he were kidding. "Sounds like you grew up in Dorkville. What did you do?"

"Read books, did chores, homework."

"Bo-o-o-r-ing!!"

His mom had been thrilled with the carpet they'd ordered from the Sears Roebuck catalog. Now, near the doors, the rug was worn to its jute backing. A frayed path led from the La-Z-Boy to the kitchen.

He looked at the speckled gray linoleum on the kitchen floor, worn away to black near the counter and, directly under the sink, rotten wood showed through.

There was a prune-shaped spot on the enamel rim of the kitchen sink that exposed dark gray metal. She used to stand at the sink, peeling potatoes, scrubbing pans, desperately holding on.

They walked down the short hall, past the bathroom with its ancient four-legged tub that had been, at first, too tall for him to climb into without his mom's help. Later, he liked to lie in warm water, wrap his toes around the beaded chain, pull out the rubber stopper and watch the water whirlpool down the drain. After years of his mother's pleading, his old man added a pipe with a showerhead and a flimsy chrome metal curtain rod for a plastic shower curtain.

He led William past his parent's bedroom to the narrow staircase that his mom had climbed each night to tuck them into bed, say their prayers and kiss them goodnight. Their old man never bothered to say goodnight.

Upstairs, two cots with metal frames, wire springs, thin

mattresses, and blankets were covered by matching bedspreads: "Gene Autry - King of the Singing Cowboys." William wouldn't know anything about Gene Autry. Ancient times.

"That's where I slept. Cody slept over there." He pointed to a large braided oval rug that separated the beds. "Mom made that rug from our worn-out clothes."

"Worn-out clothes? You're kidding."

"We had to make do with whatever we had."

"I'll sleep in your old bed." The boy threw his bag on the other bed as the bell tolled.

"Beat you to dinner!" William raced downstairs.

Justin walked to the window, leaned against the frame and rubbed dust off the glass. He looked out at the driveway, but only saw his own reflection.

Chapter 15

Justin walked downstairs to his parents' bedroom and took a new shirt from his suitcase. He raised it to his face and inhaled, savoring its starchy freshness. Everything would be all right. He put the shirt on and then walked toward Cody's cabin for dinner. Otto charged off the porch growling and barking and forced Justin to stop until Cody came to the door and called off the damned dog.

They sat at the small round dinner table near the wood cook stove. Cody said grace and then Linda passed the food family style. The sheen of grease on the fried chicken made him wish he were dining in one of his favorite Manhattan restaurants.

William asked how cold it got during the winter.

"Twenty to thirty below. We get lots of snow. It gets rough, but you sorta get used to it," Cody said.

"I don't. It would be nice to spend the winter in town where it's warmer and there are people around," Linda said.

"Yeah, well you know that's not possible. Besides, I've got the stock to feed," Cody said.

A rough-edged silence fell as they ate.

Finally Cody turned to Justin, "Had any thoughts about how to save our place?"

"What have you and Dad done?" Justin asked.

"Dad wanted to handle it. I respected that. He drove all over creation asking other ranchers for help. He tried everything."

William asked for another piece of fried chicken. Linda passed him the platter and he picked out a leg.

"Did our old man talk with Sara about a loan?" Justin asked.

"Yep, but not at first. She was a rich outsider and he didn't want to be beholden to a neighbor taking advantage," Cody said.

"How could they take advantage?" Will asked.

"Well, like having leverage to run their cows on our allotment, and then there was all that enviro bullshit she promotes," Cody said.

Linda spoke up, "Now cut that out, Cody. She's a friend."

"Yeah. You're right. Anyway, Sara put a conservation easement on their place. She claimed it was to prevent future development. But that was bull, the real reason was to get a tax break," Cody said.

"Did she tell you that?" Justin asked.

"No, but it doesn't take a rocket scientist to figure that out. And then she got on the Montana board of that Nature Conservancy and she tried to talk us into putting on an easement," Cody said.

"I think our old man might have considered it if The Nature Conservancy offered to pay up hard cash for our development rights, but she said they didn't have money on hand and it would take time to raise it, so it would be best for us to take a deduction off our taxes. Hell, we didn't have anything to deduct from. Besides, our old man hated outsiders telling us what to do with our land and he hated commie bureaucrats telling us how to run our lives. Nobody knows better than a rancher how to conserve his land."

Cody took a pinch of chew from his tobacco can and jammed it between his teeth and cheek.

Linda got up and cleared the dishes. William surprised Justin by helping her.

"Why do you think they are commies?" Justin asked.

"He doesn't," Linda said. "He's just spouting his daddy's

line. Cody, why don't you tell Justin what he wants to know?"

He rubbed his head with the stump of his thumb and then folded his arms across his chest and gave her an angry look.

"Which is?"

"What did Sara tell your Daddy?"

"Just like you, Justin, she claimed her personal money was tied up, like in a trust, and she couldn't swing a loan, and then she started on that enviro bullshit again. She thought she might get The Nature Conservancy to redeem the mortgage until they found a conservation buyer. But having a new owner would be no different than losing our land to the bank."

"I'll talk with Sara. Maybe I can change her mind," Justin said.

"Sure you can." Cody spit tobacco juice into a plastic bottle, set it on the table.

Linda asked William to take the garbage out to the trash can behind the cabin.

"Did Dad have a life insurance policy?" Justin asked.

"He did, but he let the policy lapse when he took bankruptcy."

"He must have been at the end of his rope," Justin said.

"Wouldn't you be?"

"Depressed enough to drive off that cliff?" Justin asked.

"Oh hell no! He wasn't that bad. He either passed out with a stroke or something, or maybe a front tie-rod busted." Cody stirred a spoonful of sugar into his coffee. The spoon clinked hollow against the cup. "But I told you there were other tire tracks at the scene. Looked like one truck braked and another spun its tires."

"Like someone pushed our old man off the edge?" Justin asked.

"Oh, Cody is always thinking the worst. Why, he's the most paranoid man I ever met," Linda said.

Later that night, Justin took two sleeping pills. He prayed sleep would arrive before the nightmare. In each dream, the beast got closer to killing him. Would he die during the next nightmare, in the dream? He'd heard the old superstition that in a dream, if you fell and hit bottom without first waking, you'd die in real life. Which was reality, the nightmares or the daydreams? The nightmare bear had followed him to Manhattan and appeared after he thought about the ranch and his old man and the shed. Maybe tonight the drugs would knock him out before the bear came out of hiding.

He climbed into bed. Before turning off the lamp, he looked at the silver-framed picture of his mother, a pretty young woman smiling at him across lost years. He studied the picture carefully, trying to figure out some things about his mom, and maybe himself in the process. But he couldn't. His mom just kept moving further and further away from him and back into time.

His eyes fluttered shut. Blood pounded through his temples. The dream was always the same.

He was a small boy again. He stood in his pajamas at the window looking down at the shed. Light from the lantern seeped through cracks between the boards. He knew the bear was inside. It would come for him. His fingers gripped the window frame. It pushed the door open. The light cast a black shadow across the earth. The shadow moved. Its massive head appeared. Saliva hung from its mouth, reflected by lantern light, gently swinging back and forth, a hypnotic movement of silver against black. The beast stopped. It didn't need to look up at him standing in the window because it knew he was there. Then it moved toward the house.

He turned to warn his brother, but Cody and the beds and the bedside tables and the dresser and the rug between the beds had disappeared. He was alone.

He heard wooden boards creak as the beast climbed the

stairs. The bedroom door creaked opened. The stairwell's light bulb cast dim light into the room. A black shadow crept across the floor and slid up the wall. He smelled the beast's fetid breath. He looked for escape, but the room had changed – there were no windows, no doors – only a long bare corridor.

A dish-scooped head emerged from behind the door. Its eyes locked on him. The hair on its shoulder hump ruffed. Fangs glistened. It shook its head. Saliva exploded from its jaws.

Justin fled — his feet pounded the hardwood floor machine-gun fast. Behind him, the bear's rolling gait quickened to a trot, its voice a deep huffing. The floor morphed from hardwood into soft earth and then into swamp. Muck sucked at his feet. He fled in slow motion while the bear skimmed the swamp's surface, gaining without effort.

Justin strained to gain speed, even though he knew speed meant nothing. He felt the bear's breath on his back, prolonging the chase to savor the kill.

There was no end to the room, no escape but up toward the ceiling. He flapped his arms and felt the friction of heavy air against his hands. He flailed his arms. He kicked to free his feet. His left foot pulled out and then his right foot sucked from the mud with a hollow plop.

The sound enraged the beast. It roared and snapped its great jaws together with short hard clacks. And then it charged for the kill.

Justin's body rose. He was flying. The bear reached for him, but he twisted horizontal, barely escaping the claws. He flapped his arms even harder and he rose in slow motion.

The bear stood on its hind legs, claws reaching.

Justin's back bumped against the ceiling. He sucked in his belly and pressed against the ceiling.

Ivory-tipped claws sliced inches from him, each swipe a swooshing sound. He held his breath. Claws ribboned his pajamas.

The jaws opened . . . saliva dripped . . . claws tore.

Justin moaned as he rode the drugs into a dreamless sleep.

Chapter 16

The next morning, Justin woke to the sound of the bell. He stared at the ceiling and thought about the damned nightmare.

He dressed and walked to the living room that smelled like charred logs. He'd forgotten to tell William that he'd helped build the stove by spot-welding a smaller steel barrel inside a larger barrel. The air space between the drums created heat that escaped into the room through vents cut into the sides of the outer barrel.

His old man let him weld a flat metal sheet on top so they could heat water and coffee. Justin was proud of his work. His old man had said, "It'll do."

He noticed a red coffee can on top of the woodstove. Curious, he shook it. It sounded like the can held dry dirt with pebbles, definitely not coffee. He held his breath and pried off the plastic top. Its gray contents contained tiny pieces of bone.

Cody was one sick son-of-a-bitch.

He jammed the lid back on and then dropped the can on the stovetop. He walked to the bottom of the stairwell and called to William. There was no answer. He climbed the stairs to the bedroom. It was empty, which was strange because the boy hated getting up early.

Returning downstairs, he grabbed a jacket and stepped onto the porch. The shed squatted thirty-three steps east. Lord knows how many times he'd counted those footsteps. His hands shook.

He closed his eyes, sucked in bitter mountain air and then walked toward Cody's cabin, where smoke curled from the chimney. He heard raucous calls. High overhead, a pair of Sandhill Cranes rode a thermal current, spiraling high into a brittle sky.

He was close to the other cabin when the damned dog charged off the porch, barking and growling. He stopped until Otto circled behind him and then he rushed up the steps and opened the cabin door to a flood of aromas — frying bacon and baked bread — and the sound of a TV.

Linda opened the wood stove's warming oven and took out a platter of pancakes. She noticed Justin, picked up the remote and turned off the TV.

"Good morning. Sleep well?"

"Have you seen William?"

"That boy of yours was sitting on the front porch before daylight, waiting for Cody. He drank a cup of hot chocolate while Cody had his coffee. William discovered our satellite internet connection was down and darned if he didn't up and fix it. We've tried and tried and couldn't. The service people were going to charge us an arm and leg to drive up here to fix it. Cody was impressed."

"So am I," Justin said.

"Anyway, after that they left for chores. William's so enthusiastic," Linda said

"It'll wear off."

"Maybe," Linda's voice trailed off.

"Actually, I'm happy he's interested in something other than computer games." He looked out the window at the shed.

She handed him a cup and grabbed a hot-pad, picked up the coffee pot and began to pour. She stopped. "Your hands are shaking."

"I'm cold," he lied. He used both hands to pick up the cup.

He got it to his lips without spilling and ignored Linda's inquisitive look. He was thankful she didn't pry.

They heard laughter. The door swung open. Cody and William stomped in and hung up their coats.

"Take off your boots in the house," Cody ordered.

The boy used the boot rack and then ran into the kitchen.

"Dad! You should have been with us! It was wild! Uncle Cody and I walked up to the pasture and he whistled and the horses galloped toward us like crazy and I thought they were going to run over us but Uncle Cody told me to stand still next to him and the horses ran up to us and then they stopped and I got to pet one's nose and then another one bit his behind and he reared and spun and they galloped past us down the road and into the corral where they ran around kicking and bucking until we brought the bucket of oats out and poured oats into trays and then we watched them push each other away from their trays and Uncle Cody explained about the pecking order — how the toughest pushed the others away, but they finally settled down and found his own tray of oats and they munched them up and then they walked to the water trough and drank and then they walked into the middle of the corral and laid down and rolled on their backs and over again and then stood up and shook the dust off and then just stood there like they were ready to fall asleep. Boy, it was insane!"

"That's great."

He'd never heard his son gush a torrent of words, never heard him let down from his city schoolboy pseudo-sophistication, never before watched him act with childlike enthusiasm.

Cody and William washed their hands in the kitchen sink.

Linda shook her head. "I've tried to teach your brother to wash up in the bathroom, but he's a slow learner."

Cody grinned and tossed William a dishtowel. They sat down.

"Shall we?" Cody took their hands and bowed his head.

William had been uncomfortable during last night's dinner prayer, but this morning he bowed his head and said a loud "Amen."

"Dive in, boys!" Cody reached for the bacon.

William watched Cody grab at his fork with his deformed hand and then said, "After breakfast, Uncle Cody is going to teach me how to ride."

"I'll teach you."

Justin ignored Cody's look and vowed to do a better job than his old man had done with him.

"But Cody said he would."

"A father teaches his son how to ride. Cody can watch."

"That's right. It's a father's job." Cody took a pinch of chew.

Justin walked to the woodstove and poured another cup of coffee. He turned to them. "What's the deal with the coffee can on our stove?"

Linda and William looked at Cody.

"Dad's ashes," Cody said.

"In a coffee can?"

Cody slid the chair back and crossed his legs. "Well, Sam Dolan, he's the funeral director, he asked if we wanted an urn. I told him Dad had no use for anything fancy. So Sam put Dad's ashes in a plain black plastic box, about so big." He used his hands to show the size of the box. "Well, I brought him home and decided he'd be happiest if he was near the woodstove that you and him built."

He leaned forward, spit tobacco juice in the bottle and then picked up his cup and drained the coffee. Linda walked to the stove, refilled the cup and put it on the table in front of Cody. Justin watched steam rise from the cup.

"Since no one was using that stove, I put Dad on top. That didn't look right, so I pondered about what he liked to do sitting in front of the stove. He drank whiskey in the early days, but later on he just drank coffee. I knew he wouldn't like to be packed in a black plastic box, so I thought it fitting to put him in that Folger's can until you and me could spread him together."

That was the last damned thing Justin wanted to do. Cody could spread their old man's ashes by himself, anywhere he wanted — flush him down the toilet for all he cared. He turned away and dumped the remains of his coffee in the sink and put the cup on the counter.

Cody said, "I know where we could spread his ashes. Dad always talked about our last elk hunt together up on the crest above Lost Man's Trailhead."

That had been a fiasco. Their old man had ordered Justin to shoot the biggest bull, Cody to shoot the second. Justin aimed for a quick-kill neck shot. Just as he squeezed the trigger, the bull dropped his head to feed. His bullet missed. Later, he had to listen to the old man brag to everyone about how Cody had to shoot both bulls.

Justin leaned against the kitchen counter. "Thought when you built this new cabin, you would have torn down the old shed."

Cody squinted at him over the rim of his coffee cup.

"Built an outside room on the side of this place for the tools and firewood. More convenient. Nothing left in the old one."

"Really?" Justin said, hating the sarcasm in his voice.

Cody turned in his chair and grinned at him. "You spent more time than me in that shed."

Chapter 17

After breakfast, they walked to the barn and into the aromas of hay and leather. Justin handed William a halter and several oat cubes and then they moved into the corral where the horses stood. Baily was asleep, lying down on the far side of the rest of the horses. Justin told the boy to stay close as he moved at an unhurried pace through the herd toward Baily.

"See how the other horses watch us? They know we're not after them, so they'll step out of our way." He felt the boy's shoulder tight against his arm. They wove their way through the horses until they stood several feet from the sleeping horse.

Baily raised his head from the dirt, eyed them and then rolled to his side, reached forward with his front legs, rocked to a standing position, shook dirt off his body, creating a dust cloud, and then walked away.

William started to follow. Justin put his hand on the boy's arm to stop him. "Wait for the horse to stop and look at you, then hold out the cube so he can see you have a treat for him."

Baily stopped, looked back, spotted the cube and then walked toward them. He stretched his head toward William's hand, lips munching. The horse's nose touched the boy's hand. William jerked his hand away. The cube fell to the dirt. Baily spun away.

"Don't pull your hand away so fast," Justin said.

"He was going to bite me."

He taught the boy how to balance the cube on a flattened palm, thumb held close against the first finger so not to be nipped and then to wait for the horse to take the cube. William was successful the second time. He smiled.

"Now offer him a second cube, but this time hold it out to your side and when Baily touches the cube, slip the halter rope over the top of his neck and hold him."

William complied. Justin showed him how to slip the halter over the horse's nose and behind the ears and then tie the throat latch around the neck.

They tied the horse to a hitching rail near the barn. Justin began brushing the horse. "Baily is a quarter horse. He stands about fifteen three hands tall."

"What's a quarter horse?" William asked.

"It's the breed of horses that are good for working cattle and trail riding. There are other kinds of horses: thoroughbreds for racing, Arabians for endurance, draft horses for pulling heavy loads, and gaited horses like Tennessee Walkers or Fox Trotters that have smooth paces."

"So what's the difference?" William asked.

"Conformation. A good quarter horse has powerful hind-quarters." He ran his hand over Baily's hips and then pointed to the lower part of the leg just above the hoof.

"I like a horse with long pasterns that can soften the impact and give a smooth ride. Short pasterns make the hoof point down, so the horse has a short stride and gives a jarring trot like sitting on a jack hammer."

"Uh-huh."

Cody walked out of the barn. "Baily has cow sense. He knows how to move cattle without guidance. My girls moved a lot of cows on him. You can trust him. He'll take care of you."

Justin taught the boy how to saddle the horse, making certain the cinch was just right.

"Make it too loose and the saddle will slip when you mount

and you'll roll under and the horse will buck. If the cinch is too tight it might cut off blood in a vein and the horse could pass out with you on top."

William looked uncertain.

They led Baily to the arena and he instructed the boy how to bridle, how to use his fingers to open the mouth and how to make certain not to let the steel bit hit the horse's teeth. He taught William how to mount, holding the reins in the left hand, placing that hand not on the horn, because the saddle might slip, but on top of the horse's neck, and then placing the right hand on the back of the saddle to help lift. He showed him how to hold the reins — not too tight, but not so loose that the horse couldn't be pulled to a stop. William was a quick learner, which surprised and pleased Justin.

"Sit proud when you're in the saddle — shoulders square, back straight."

Same thing his old man had told him, but he'd be damned if he'd do what his old man had done to him.

William sat the saddle well and held the reins properly. Justin took the halter rope and led the horse and William around and around the arena. Finally, he taught the boy to use the reins to turn the horse to the left and to the right, to stop and to back up.

"If Baily runs away with you or begins to buck, you'll need to get him under control. Hold onto the saddle horn and then pull one rein back to your knee to force the horse to spin until it stops. Got it?"

"I hope so," William said with an unsure voice.

"Comfortable now?" Justin asked.

"No," the boy looked scared.

There were other things to show the boy, like putting pressure on the legs to guide the horse into a turn, but there was plenty of time to teach the finer points of riding. He took off the halter rope.

"I'll walk next to you. I'll tell you what to do and you do what I say."

"But . . ."

"I'll be right here if you need help." He stepped to the side and the horse stood still. "Use your heels to nudge him in the ribs."

William held the reins with his left hand. His right hand gripped the saddle horn. The boy's eyes were wide with fear.

"Go ahead and kick him in the side with your heels."

"I don't know . . ."

"It's all right. I'm right here for you," Justin said.

William gave a soft kick. Baily didn't move. William kicked harder. Baily stepped forward at a slow walk. William grinned at his Dad.

An hour later, William was safe enough to let Justin sit on the corral fence and watch. He had to keep reminding the boy to hold the correct length of reins — he'd either hold too tight, backing up the horse, or too loose and Baily would begin to trot. After a couple of hours, William got the drift of riding and began to enjoy himself.

After he was confident the boy could handle the horse, he climbed outside the corral fence and hooked his elbows on the top rail.

"Keep a loose rein and kick him when he tries to stop."

He remembered he had been four or five, legs too short for his feet to reach the stirrups, when his old man threw him on a saddle, tossed him the reins, shouted "Yee-aw!" and slapped the horse on the butt. The horse spurted forward. Justin had dropped the reins and clutched the saddle horn with both hands while the horse trotted across the arena. He bounced from one side of the saddle to the other, holding on in sheer terror. Near the end of the corral, the horse stepped on a rein, bucked and threw Justin high over its neck onto the dirt where he lay on his back and sobbed.

His old man shouted, "You got the falling off part down good. Now stop sniveling and bring that horse back here. You're getting back on."

Justin watched his son nudge the horse into a trot and before he could tell William how to move in the saddle, the boy sat the saddle with the rhythm of the horse. Grinning like crazy, William soon had the horse trotting around the arena. The kid was doing well. Very well.

Cody walked over and stood next to Justin, "You taught your boy good. You were a hell-of-a lot better on this ranch than you gave yourself credit for. Good you came home."

"This isn't my home," Justin said.

Cody arced juice over the fence rails and then turned toward Justin. "Best you got out, but now that's over and done with. Time to move on."

"To what?"

"Your choice, but you don't have a future if you don't make amends with the past," Cody said.

Justin cast a sideways glance at his brother. "Easy for you to say."

Cody shrugged.

William reined Baily into a slow figure eight and then walked to the fence.

"How'd I do?"

"You're a natural." Justin rubbed the horse's forehead.

"What do you think, Uncle Cody?"

Cody took off his hat, scratched the top of his head with his thumb and then settled the Stetson tight. "Well, I think you done good, Will."

"Really?"

"His name is William," Justin said.

"That's a stuffy name. Might be okay for New York City, but not out here."

Cody turned to the boy. "Okay with you if I call you Will?"

The boy blinked and looked down at the reins before looking at his uncle. "I'd like that. A lot." He gave his Dad a tight-lipped smile.

Justin ignored both of them and said it was time to unsaddle.

After they unsaddled and brushed Baily, Justin showed the boy how to trim the horse's matted mane using electric trimmers.

"Now Baily's mane looks just like Uncle Cody's crew cut," Will said.

Justin picked up the trimmer and reached for the boy's arm. "I'll give you a crew cut."

Will laughed and spun out of reach.

Cody introduced them to Jake, a gelding out of Princess, the mare that had once been Justin's horse.

"He's your horse, Justin. If you want, you can ride Jake while you're here," Cody said.

Justin had no intentions of riding a horse, but he thanked his brother for the offer.

As they walked back toward Cody's cabin for lunch, Justin decided that he wasn't going to start World War III over the kid's name. He'd use whatever name his son wanted.

After lunch, they walked to their cabin while Cody took a nap.

"What did Grandmother look like?" Will asked.

"There's a picture of her inside."

Justin led the boy into the bedroom, took the photograph off the dresser and they sat on the bed to look at her.

"She was pretty." Will pointed to a silver locket she wore from a silver chain around her neck. "What's that?"

"Her mother's locket. She kept a picture of your great grandmother in it."

"Your Mom looks about Mom's age."

Justin studied the picture — he hadn't made the connection.

"And you were my age when she left?"

"Yes."

"Why did she leave?"

"I don't know."

"Did you do something to make her go?" Will asked.

"I used to think so. I always wondered if I had done something to push her away. It hurt a lot and I still miss her."

"Where did she go?"

"I don't know. Everyone searched for her, but she just disappeared. My father said she left with another man."

"Huh."

"It's your mom's new job, you know. Her job forced her to open an office in London. You didn't make her leave. I hope you don't think you did anything."

Will shrugged and slid off the bed. "I'm going up to my room."

Justin put the photo on the dresser and stared at it for a moment longer. He walked outside and gazed at the shed. Otto eyed him from Cody's porch, but at least the damned dog didn't charge him and bark his fool head off.

He walked along the riverbank and watched the currents swirl and eddy. He found a sunny place and sat down. The valley was different than he'd remembered, so was the ranch. The river was the same, yet altered by relentless currents. He'd changed since leaving. Would his homecoming create other changes?

Lying in the grass, he inhaled forgotten scents — pine trees and fresh-turned earth. Swallows swooped through the sky, chasing insects invisible to his eye. A green dragonfly materialized inches above his face, hovering, darting, hovering, and then swooping to catch a fly. He closed his eyes. A horse neighed. Another answered. The sun was warm. His eyes fluttered shut and he fell into a dreamless sleep.

Sometime later, a cawing raven woke Justin. It was time to talk to Sara.

Chapter 18

Justin decided to take William with him to Sara's, hoping the boy's presence would neutralize a potentially emotional scene. He walked into his cabin and up to the upstairs bedroom. William lay on the bed reading a book.

He couldn't believe the boy wasn't playing his computer game. Wonders never ceased.

"Aunt Linda gave me a book about horses that her kids had read when they were my age."

They drove over to the Parson Ranch. He hoped Sara's husband, Frank Sterling, would not be there. This would be complicated enough without a husband looking on. He wondered if her husband had been that young guy he'd seen her saying goodbye to after the funeral.

He turned off the county road, drove through the Parson Ranch gate and continued down a long gravel driveway that wove through a stand of pines until they approached a new log barn and corrals. The place was immaculate. A narrower road forked to the right and disappeared in the trees. He assumed it led to their new house.

They parked near the barn and spotted Sara in the round pen working a young horse. She stood in the center of the ring, erect and focused on the horse that trotted circles around her. A silver belly Stetson shaded her eyes as she turned, first one side of her body highlighted by the afternoon sun and then her other side, breasts and hips dancing in and out of sunlight and shadow. Her hair swung with her body's movement. She seemed graceful and confident.

"What's she doing with that whip?" Will asked

"She uses it to keep the horse moving in circles," Justin whispered. "We have to be quiet, so the horse doesn't get distracted. Horses move away from pressure, so she snaps the end of the whip towards its hindquarters to keep it moving at a good pace."

"Does she hit it?" William asked as they moved closer to the round pen.

"Never. She'd never use that whip to strike a horse."

They walked to the round pen. Justin touched his river stone and looked over the fence, while William watched between the wooden rails.

Sara turned, facing the horse as it trotted around the edge of the pen. She gave them a quick, annoyed glance. "Can't talk now."

The trotting horse slowed when it approached Justin and William. The horse's eyes rolled, eyeing them. Sara took two quick steps forward and snapped the whip close behind its hindquarters. It broke into a canter and turned its attention back to her.

She glanced at them again. "Lost?" She either didn't recognize him or pretended not to.

"Maybe, but I know where I am," Justin said.

Will glanced up at him through his bangs.

"The Thatcher ranch is twenty miles further up valley." She turned with the horse, away from him.

"We're looking for Sara Sterling," he said.

She glanced over her shoulder and watched him throughout the turn.

"You!"

"And my son, William."

"Will," the boy said with force.

"You're too late," she said.

"That's what everyone tells me."

"Everyone can't be wrong." Her voice was cold as she turned with the horse.

"Don't count on it," he said.

"That figures. This is going take a long time. Call if you want an appointment."

"We'll wait," Justin said.

The horse stalled to a walk. Sara lunged forward, snapping the whip close to its tail, snapping it again and again until the horse leapt into a canter. She snapped the whip behind the animal and it galloped in circles until white froth dripped from its mouth and it heaved gasping spurts of breath. White sweat formed on the horse's shoulders and flanks.

"Horses are one of the few animals that can sweat," Justin whispered.

Sara was breathing heavily. When the horse settled down into a fast trot and licked its lips, she backed off.

Will dug the toe of his boot into the loose dirt and pushed the dirt into different shapes, walls, piles and holes.

During the next half hour, they watched her gain the horse's attention and finally, the horse stopped and looked at her, his ears forward. She moved toward the horse and he stood firm. Her domination of the animal was complete. Her self-assurance and control were traits he'd not witnessed before. That made her even more appealing. There was a certainty in her manner and in her attitude that reminded him of how he behaved during a business deal.

Soon the horse followed her around the round pen like a well-trained dog.

"They call that 'hooked-on'," he told William. "The horse trusts her and she has its attention."

They watched her lead the gelding through a gate into the big corral. She patted its hindquarter and the horse moved off, dropped to its knees and then rolled in the dust.

Sara walked toward them and tucked the whip under her left arm. She took off her hat, pulled back her hair, wiped a thin sheen of perspiration from her forehead and then settled the Stetson business-like over her eyes. She slipped through the gate. Justin smelled her sweat – not a fresh sweet scent, but a robust aroma of physical labor.

He introduced William, who shook her hand and reminded him that he preferred to be called "Will." Her smile was wonderful, but it faded when she turned toward him.

"Good to see you again, Sara," Justin said.

"What business?" she asked.

He told her about the mortgage redemption deadline and asked if she'd consider helping.

"I talked with your Dad about doing something with The Nature Conservancy, but he refused. You're rich. You buy the certificate back," she said.

"My money is tied up in my business."

"Well, I'm certain you can figure it out. I have to go." She turned toward the barn.

"I'm sorry I didn't write."

She spun toward them. "I don't know what you're talking about."

Will looked at Sara and then Justin.

"I didn't answer your letters."

"We were just friends. We were young. It didn't matter."

He didn't want their exchange to end this way.

Face frozen, she turned to Will, "I'm sorry if I seem rude, but it's been a long day."

Desperate to keep the conversation going, he said, "Does your husband like it here?

Her eyes widened. "He's gone."

"Gone where?"

She raised the whip and then froze.

He stepped back as if she'd struck him.

"Fuck you and the horse you rode in on, Justin Thatcher."

"Wow!" Will said. "Over the top!"

They watched her stride away.

During the drive back to the ranch, Will alternately played his video game and glanced at him, waiting for an explanation about Sara's reaction, but embarrassed to ask.

Justin replayed the scene again and again, trying to figure out what had happened. As far as women were concerned, he seemed to be snake-bit. He remembered sneaking out of Red's apartment the other night and then standing under the "Jesus Saves" neon sign. If women didn't dump him, he dumped them. He wondered if the trauma of his mother's leaving had left a scar that prevented him from having a normal relationship with a woman.

Chapter 19

Back at the ranch, Linda raked the lawn, while Cody tossed debris into the dump truck. They would want to know what happened, but Justin didn't know what could have made Sara so angry. He wasn't sure what he would say until Will jumped out of the car. "Guess what? Sara swore at Dad. It was so cool!"

He wanted to wring the kid's neck. He got out and walked over to them.

"What did you do to deserve that?" Linda demanded.

"Nothing."

"Dad wanted to know if her husband liked it here."

"Oh, shit!" Cody looked at Linda.

"What?" Justin asked.

"Frank died five years ago," Cody said.

"Died? Why the hell didn't you tell me?" Justin asked.

"I was going to when we passed her place, but Will saw that herd of elk and after that, I guess it slipped my mind."

Linda leaned on the rake, "Sara and Frank were alone on a pack trip up in the wilderness and his horse spooked. Bucked him off. He hit his head on a rock and he died right there. She couldn't go for help lest a bear would find him. Somehow she got his body up across the saddle, roped it on and led the horse back down to the trailhead."

"I'll call to apologize," Justin said.

"She might not believe you. I'll call her." Linda walked into their cabin.

Justin walked over to the riverbank and looked at the current. A cottonwood leaf, yellow and curled, floated downstream. It skimmed the surface, racing toward a seam between the current and a back eddy that formed behind a boulder. The leaf surfed the seam, slid down the inside lip into the lazy pool. Trapped, the leaf whirled slowing circles until it stopped dead. Water seeped over its edges, suffocating it, dragging it under. It sank into a graveyard of its brethren, soft, black and decaying.

He shivered.

A few minutes later, Linda returned. "I told Sara you didn't know about Frank. She's embarrassed. She wants you to go down there now to talk it out before she comes up to dinner."

He took a quick shower, dressed and put on a new shirt. At this rate, he'd run out of clean shirts. He'd have to buy new ones when he drove to town to talk with Miss Adams. Sam's Boots would be the only place in Cora that might carry shirts, but they wouldn't have the kind he needed – new, white, starched. They would only have denim or cotton cowboy shirts. They wouldn't smell the same as those to which he'd grown accustomed. Relied upon. He counted his remaining shirts again. If he left for Manhattan immediately after visiting Miss Adams, he might get back to his supply.

Thirty minutes later, he knocked on the massive plank door of Sara's lodge, prepared to apologize for his innocent insult. He'd grovel, but not for long.

The door opened. She stood barefooted, toenails painted bright green. The collar of her white shirt was turned up, drawing his eyes to the hollow of her throat where his lips had felt her moans rise before he had heard them. She'd left the top three buttons of the shirt undone, revealing smooth skin that he had loved to caress. The scent of her freshly washed hair bridged their awkward silence, the fragrance triggering old memories.

"Are you going to invite me in?"

She blinked as if awaking from a trance. "I suppose it would be rude to slam the door in your face after I invited you here to apologize."

He stepped forward, but she blocked his way.

"I'm sorry, I . . ."

She cut him off. "You have no idea what it means to be sorry, but for what it's worth, I'm sorry too."

"Cody hadn't told me your husband had died. I didn't mean to hurt you."

"I don't imagine you ever intended to hurt me."

He smelled the freshness of her breath. "So, apologies accepted. Is that it?"

"That depends on what you want."

"I know what I want, Sara. Do you?"

Her eyes flashed. He couldn't tell if it was anger or something else – desire? A challenge?

"I have what I want. Do you?" She smiled and turned and then walked away, bare feet skimming across the flagstone foyer.

He stood at the partially open door, watching her, uncertain, and unnerved by his uncertainty. He grasped the doorframe, hesitant to cross the threshold. Anger rose at this hesitancy – he'd never been afraid of business risks – yet now he was indecisive. He'd apologized. She'd accepted. That's what he'd come to do. They'd cleared the air and they'd see each other tonight at dinner. He turned to leave and then remembered Cody's remark about not having a future until reconciling with the past. He'd apologized to Sara, but not reconciled. He walked across the threshold to follow her.

A massive river rock fireplace anchored the far end of the great room with a high peaked ceiling and massive log beams. The floors were wide pine planks softened by Navajo rugs. There were two groupings of leather couches and chairs, with a long couch in front of the fireplace. An immense white sheepskin rug lay on the floor in front of the couch. Stuffed trophy heads adorned the walls — a seven point bull elk, a mule deer buck with massive antlers, a moose, a black bear, a grizzly, a full curl Rocky Mountain bighorn ram and a cougar.

Sara waited for him at a copper-topped bar, two glasses of red wine in her hands. Her certainty bothered him — she knew he'd follow her. She offered him a glass.

He raised his glass. "Here's to the past and to the future."

"Here's to now," she said.

They clinked and then sipped their wine without taking their eyes from the other. She waited for him to say something.

He nodded to the stuffed animals. "Nice trophies. Your husband must have enjoyed hunting."

"They're mine. I enjoy the challenge of a hunt."

He studied the trophies. "It looks like you've taken a mature male of every species that lives in this area. Have your sights on anything else?"

"I'm waiting for a challenge."

"Are you interested in younger ones?"

"Younger what?"

"Animals . . . men?"

Her eyes danced over a smile. "Well, that depends on the circumstances. What about you?"

"Me?"

"Linda told me you're divorced. Are you dating?"

"I wouldn't call it dating."

"Sport fucking?"

"More like your trophy hunting. There's no challenge after you bag one."

She took his wine glass and put it with hers on the bar and then she moved close. She touched his chest with her fingertips and then grabbed his hair and pulled down until their lips met.

Her lips tasted the way he'd remembered, full and wet and

responsive. Her breath the same as he'd imagined. He tipped her chin up and kissed the hollow in her neck with its warm scent that promised other pleasures, a scent that recalled other times, good times.

She raised his head and kissed him with a passion he'd almost forgotten. And then she pushed him away. "That's enough."

He reached for her.

She smiled and spun away.

Confused, he watched her walk toward the foyer. He followed her to the front door that she held open. "What was that all about?"

"We both wondered if it would be better than before."

"It's too early to tell," he said.

"Let's get something straight, Justin. We were kids and we had a summer fling. You went your way. I went mine. It's been twenty-eight years. We can't turn back the clock."

"But we . . ."

She hushed him by touching her fingers to his lips. "I was perfectly happy before you intruded upon my life, and I'll be perfectly happy when you go back to New York. I'm not looking for a man and I certainly don't want to try to recreate a childish fling with you."

"That sounds like an ultimatum."

"Those are my terms," she said and led him to the door. "I need to get ready. See you at dinner."

He drove back toward his ranch and smiled. She'd been much more than he'd fantasized — she'd been his equal. And more.

Chapter 20

An hour later, he'd showered again, changed shirts and dressed for dinner. He walked out to the front porch to wait for Sara. He sat in a rocking chair and tried to figure out what the heck was going on. His encounters with her had been a surprise. His memories had been of their physical relationship. She had been his first lover and he'd acted like a bull elk in rut. Now he saw that she was an engaging, likable woman. Smart. His equal mentally and verbally, and perhaps more than his equal psychologically. He was now fascinated with the total woman, not just her body. She'd make a worthy opponent or ally.

Bathed in sunlight, the shed looked picturesque, even benign. What happened inside . . . he didn't want to think about that . . . he squeezed his river stone.

Instead, he concentrated on a robin that hopped across the grass. The bird stopped, cocked its head to listen for a worm, pecked and then hopped to a new hunting ground. The robin chirped and then flew toward him. It perched on the railing directly in front of him. The bird stared at him as though he was a most interesting object. He tried not to move or blink or frighten it away because he welcomed its company, which struck him as strange.

The tiny black eyes bore into him. Its beak cracked open and he saw breath exhale. The red-orange feathers of its breast lay flat and smooth and plump. But the tip of its left wing feather hung askew as if broken, marring an otherwise perfect appearance.

He felt a weird sort of kinship with the bird. He raised his hand to scratch his cheek. The robin chirped and flew away and broke the spell, which he discounted as being a rather stupid stretch of his imagination.

He heard a sound of tires crunching on gravel. Sara's red pickup drove up the road past the barn, through the trees and toward the cabins. When the truck passed, he was astonished to see Sara was in the passenger seat and a young man drove her truck, the same guy she'd said a furtive goodbye to after the funeral. Why would she bring him to dinner? Where had he been when Justin visited her?

He stared at the shed without seeing it as he tried to calm his breathing and ignore the pounding in his temples.

Linda greeted Sara and the young man with hugs. Otto wagged his tail and waited to be petted. They walked inside her cabin.

Justin sat in the rocker until Will ran out of their cabin, rang the bell and ran back inside, and then he walked along the riverbank toward dinner.

The river was murky, running high, broken limbs and debris swirling in angry currents. Otto guarded the porch and bared his fangs with a low growl. He kept walking toward the dog until it finally stepped aside.

He noticed the huge elk antlers nailed above their cabin door were almost as big as those on Sara's mounted elk. He took a deep breath and walked in. The setting sun beamed through the kitchen window, a yellow shaft of light on the table. Across the room, Sara and Will huddled close together on the couch, the boy looking as though he was telling her something important. They glanced at Justin. Sara smiled. Will looked guilty.

Linda and Cody stood next to the stove with the new guy.

Cody poured Maker's Mark into a glass. He looked like he'd already had a couple. Justin walked toward them and flashed back to when his father drank whiskey. Nothing good came of that.

"Want a drink?" Cody asked.

"Think I'll have a Pepsi." Justin pulled a can from the refrigerator and popped its top.

Cody nodded toward the young man. "This is Sara's boy, Harry."

Justin heard his own breath exhale.

Harry shook his hand, his grip firm. He looked Justin in the eye. Smiled.

"I've heard a lot about you, Mr. Thatcher. I want to hear about your business."

The young man had one of those faces that looked familiar and he made a good first impression.

"Call me Justin."

Sara joined them. "Harry came out to check out a stallion I wanted to breed to my mare. He picked it up today and drove it to the ranch. Since he was here, I thought you'd like to meet each other."

"I understand you and Mom dated," Harry said.

Justin looked at Sara. "It was a high school fling."

"You were the high school kid. I was in college," Sara said.

Harry laughed. "So you dated a younger man? Oh, my god Mom, you're the previous generation's version of a cougar."

Sara's laugh seemed hollow.

"Which one of you shot that elk over the front door?" Sara asked.

"Cody shot him when we were in high school," Justin said, hoping his brother would have the good sense to keep his mouth shut about that fiasco.

"Do you find many trophies in Manhattan?" Sara asked.

Justin looked at her sparkling eyes and felt the gaze of the others. "I run into one now and then."

"Bag many?" Sara asked.

"As many as I possibly can."

Cody, Linda and Harry shot them inquisitive looks.

"And I suppose you mount them all?" Sara asked.

Linda interrupted. "What in the world are you two talking about?"

Justin nodded to Sara. "Why don't you explain it to them?"

"Why don't you? After all you're the expert." Sara's devilish grin dared him.

He coughed into his fist. "Apparently Sara's challenge is to hunt for trophy animals, bag them and then mount them as evidence of her successful hunt."

"And what about you, Justin?" Sara asked.

"My challenge is to hunt for a different kind of trophy — companies that are under-valued. I buy them, improve their bottom line and then flip them at a higher price."

"And tell us about mounting them," Sara said with relish.

"Mounting them is the best part. After the deal we print an announcement in the newspaper and then I have that engraved and framed. We call that a Tombstone. I hang them on my wall to impress guests, just like Sara has all those mounted heads in her cabin."

Sara pursed her lips and then gave Justin a wink. "Nicely said."

Linda called them to dinner. Justin waited until everyone had taken a seat at the round table and then he sat in the remaining chair with Sara to his right and Harry on his left. Will sat between Sara and Cody. Linda sat across from Justin, the window behind her framing a red sky.

Cody asked them to hold hands while he said grace. Justin held Sara's warm hand and felt life in her fingers. At the end of the prayer, she gave his hand a lingering squeeze. Her brown eyes contained the tiny gold flecks he remembered, her breath the sweet bouquet that recalled their youth. The rhythmic rising and falling of her breasts made him want to hold her again.

As they ate, Harry told Justin he worked for a software company in California. His dream was to start his own company as soon as he gained enough experience and made the right contacts.

"When I was your age, I thought I could make it on my own merit, but after I watched other successful businessmen, I realized that a combination of 'who you know' as well as 'what you know' will help you be successful," Justin said. He felt heat from Sara's leg close to his. Her fragrance held the scent of spring and new life.

Cody finished his third drink.

"Justin, why don't you just buy back the damned mortgage and then put a conservation easement on the ranch? You'd save the place and get a tax break at the same time."

"This isn't the time for this," Justin said.

"That's right, Cody. Not now," Linda said.

Cody looked at her. His jaw muscles twitched.

Sara touched Justin's arm.

"Do you have a better idea?"

"I'm working on it."

"What's wrong with Cody's suggestion?" Sara asked.

"First, my money is tied up in my business," Justin said. That was technically true, since he hadn't yet paid off the Farnsworth loan. "Second, I've got debts of my own, and third, buying this ranch would be a poor investment. Selling off lots would probably be the best strategy."

"I'll never agree to developing this place." Cody slammed his glass on the table. The stump of his thumb looked like an exclamation mark.

"What's wrong with development?" Harry asked.

Cody glared at him. "Some places are worth more than money. Besides, the whole damned country is being chopped up into little lots."

"Not around here," Linda said.

"Not yet. But look what happened to Jackson Hole and Kalispell and the areas around Missoula. Besides, the animals need the river areas," Cody said.

"My god, Cody, you're in the middle of a damned wilderness. The animals have thousands of miles to roam," Justin said.

Sara said, "The problem with that is that most development takes place in the riparian areas and those are critical migration pathways and the source of spring food for predators and ungulates. It's critical to keep these areas free from development."

"The animals can adapt," Justin said.

"Sure Dad, just like that squirrel that got flattened in front of your condo." Will's lips curled into the tightlipped smile Justin hated.

Cody dug out a pinch of chew, jammed into his lip, and stared at Justin. Linda took the pot from the woodstove and poured coffee into their cups. Justin felt Sara staring at him. He looked at the window. It now framed a black void.

He turned to Harry. "So you want to start your own business?"

Harry was eager to fill in his plans. Then he pumped Justin for advice and later, asked him for stories about his business deals. Justin talked. Sara and the others listened. Even Will acted interested.

Harry asked probing questions.

Justin avoided the other possible topics of discussion, but, nevertheless, found himself impressed with Sara's son.

After dinner Linda suggested they sit outside.

"Bring your guitar?" Cody asked Harry.

"It's in our truck." Harry went to get it.

Cody piled logs in the fire pit and sprinkled on a mixture of sawdust and diesel fuel. Its industrial stench reminded Justin of the city. Will lit it with a match and watched the fire grow, fascinated by the inferno. They pulled chairs close together and watched flames lick the sky. Sara sat between Justin and Will.

Cody and Harry played their guitars. Justin was surprised at their talent and he was amazed that he was enjoying himself. His taste ran more to hundred-piece professional orchestras.

Cody taught them songs and they sang. They were answered by a howl.

Will peered into the dusk. "Is that the wolf, Uncle Cody?"

"Sounds like a wolf — don't know if it's *the* wolf."

"Are the foals safe?" Linda asked.

"The mares are in the loafing sheds with the foals. They'll be fine."

The wolf howled again. Cody howled back. The wolf answered.

"Try it, Will," Justin said.

Will shook his head and put his hands beneath his armpits.

After a moment of silence, Cody said, "Let me show you how to do it."

Several minutes later, Will cupped his hands around his mouth and howled a mournful hollow sound that rose and drifted into the dark. The wolf responded. Will's teeth shone bright in the firelight. They stared at the flames.

Later, Justin taught Will how to find the North Star by tracing an imaginary line from the front edge of the Big Dipper. A satellite streaked across the sky.

Cody and Harry played some more.

"I wish I could play," Will said.

Harry handed the boy his guitar. "Use mine while you're here. I've got another guitar at home. Cody can teach you a chord or two. You can see if you like it before you buy your own."

Will grinned. He plunked the strings. The sound was terrible.

"I'll give you a lesson tomorrow," Cody said.

Harry stood up and stretched. "I'd better get home. I'm leaving tomorrow at the crack of dawn."

Sara and Justin lingered next to the fire for a moment as the others walked toward her truck.

"It was a great day," Justin said.

"What are you doing tomorrow?" Sara asked.

"I'm going to visit Miss Adams."

He'd planned to fly back to Manhattan tomorrow, but now he thought about staying another day.

"If you have time, stop by on your way back," she said.

He tried to make his voice sound flippant, "What do you have in mind this time?"

"We haven't had a chance to talk."

He laughed. "Talk was never what we did best."

"What did you think of Harry?" she asked.

"He's a great young man."

At the truck, Justin tried to kiss her cheek. She turned her head away and then shook his hand with strength that surprised him. She studied him for a moment and then said, in a low voice so the other couldn't hear, "I thought you'd like Harry. He's ours, you know."

Chapter 21

During breakfast the next morning, Linda asked Justin if he felt ill.

"I couldn't sleep last night," he said.

"Anything wrong?"

"Thinking about business," he lied.

He wondered if they knew he was Harry's father. Or had Sara been teasing? If so, that was a lot more than teasing, but he didn't remember Sara ever being cruel or malicious.

Cody said he had to check some line fences on the pastures high on Coulter Mountain. "Would you like to ride with me, Will?"

The boy's face twitched with an effort to keep from grinning.

"Sure. If that's what you want, Uncle Cody."

A few minutes later, Justin drove down the road toward Dead Man's Pass. As he approached Sara's driveway, he looked at his watch. He had plenty of time before he had to meet Miss Adams. He drove through the gate and toward the barn. She was grooming a sorrel horse inside the corral. She waved.

He waved back, parked, stepped out and took a deep breath. He walked to the corral. She slipped the halter off the horse before turning toward him. She looked lovely. He gripped the top rail. She came close and he smelled the fresh scent of shampoo. She caressed the top of his hand with her fingertips and then hooked her elbow over the railing. "On your way to visit your teacher?"

"Is Harry here?"

"He left before six."

"Oh, I forgot he planned to leave early," he lied.

"I can give you his e-mail address, if you want to get in touch."

He nodded at the horse that she'd been grooming. "Good looking mare."

"I'm going to breed her to a stallion Harry bought yesterday."

He turned and leaned back against the rail to keep his legs from shaking. Across the pasture, cottonwood trees grew tall along the banks of the river. Far beyond the river, the mountain peaks were sharply defined by an impossibly blue sky. He heard the cawing of a raven and spotted the bird sitting on the top branch pine, alone. The bird's rasping song was lonely and forlorn. Justin smelled his own scent, turned sour.

"How old is Harry?" he asked.

Her voice was steady. "His birthday is May 18th. He's twenty-seven."

"Twenty-seven?"

"I married Frank when Harry was three."

The mountains blurred. He ran his fingers through his hair and stared at his feet. His fingers sought the solace of his river stone. Black ants marched in a long single file across the ground, weaving between clumps of grass and dirt on a journey that seemed determined. At least they knew where they were going.

His voice quavered, "I don't know what to say."

"You'll think of something."

He turned and clutched the top rail and felt splinters of wood against his palms. "Why didn't you tell me?"

"Why didn't you answer my letters?

"They didn't say anything about you being pregnant." He

regretted the rough texture to his voice.

"I didn't know until after I wrote those letters. You didn't write back, so . . . " Her voice trailed off.

"You cheated me out of knowing my son."

Her eyes flashed. "I cheated you?"

"That's right!"

"How well do you know Will?"

He hurried to his car, slammed the door, started the engine and spun the tires as he turned to careen down her driveway toward the county road. When a deal goes sour, the smart man walks. He'd lived by that rule. It had served him well.

He sped down valley and then up and over Dead Man's Pass toward Cora. His breathing had calmed by the time he approached his father's marker. He stopped and looked at the spot and wondered if the financial pressures had driven the old man to commit suicide. But that didn't make sense. He simply couldn't imagine his father giving up. Maybe Cody was right, maybe something else happened.

He drove on and thought about his conversation with Sara. He'd blown it. His anger had kept him from learning what had happened, how she'd handled the pregnancy and the baby alone, the real reason she hadn't told him. If Harry had turned into a fine young man, was there hope for Will? Obviously, Sara was a better mother than Ashley, but he'd also played a part in alienating Will. He'd stop at Sara's on the way back from town and apologize.

The wailing of a siren shattered his thoughts. He realized he was driving on the paved road near the outskirts of town. He looked in his rearview mirror to see a patrol truck with its huge steel grille, strobe lights flashing. He pulled over. In the side mirror, he watched Sheriff Billy Baxter slide the truck within inches from his rear bumper. The sheriff stepped out, hitched up his gun belt and then tugged his Stetson low over his sunglasses. He walked to Justin's car. Justin rolled the window down and put his hands on the steering wheel.

The sheriff put one hand on the window frame and leaned close. "Let me ask you a question, Thatcher."

"Shoot."

"Poor choice of words."

"Get to the point."

"Going to redeem the ranch?"

"How is that your business?"

"It's a small town. You show up after all these years and everybody is asking me — is he going to redeem the ranch or is he going to flush his brother down the toilet? Done that once before when you left Cody alone with your old man out there — of course that was before your Dad sobered up."

Justin's fingers squeezed the steering wheel. "Since 'everyone' wants to know, your banker friend tells me the cost of redeeming our ranch is more than it's worth."

"You're rich. Buy it as a plaything."

"I don't like it out here," Justin said.

"Then haul your ass back to the big city."

"Not before I'm ready, Billy."

"It's Sheriff to you, Thatcher. Let me give you some advice. Drive real careful on those switchbacks. City boys like you get careless and slide off the road and end up at the bottom of the cliffs. Like what happened to your Daddy. Costs the taxpayers a lot of money to haul a body out."

"Don't want to be an expense to the taxpayers."

The sheriff got in his truck, started the diesel engine with a roar and waited. Justin pulled onto the blacktop and drove toward town. The sheriff tailgated him, steel grill guard close to his bumper. Several miles later, the sheriff finally passed, grinned and, with his fist, made the sign of a cocked gun. That gave their old friendship signal a new, ominous meaning. Justin remembered that Billy Baxter's practical jokes were humorous when they were kids. Now that he represented the law, his humor wasn't amusing — and likely wasn't meant to be funny.

As Justin continued toward town, he came to a pair of con-
clusions about the incident: first, the sheriff had pumped him
for information for the banker. The second, and even more trou-
bling, was that the sheriff might have caused his Dad's accident.

He called his investigator to find out what he'd learned
about Kurt Kamm. There was no answer. He left a message and
then looked at his watch — he still had time before he was due to
see Miss Adams. He needed fresh shirts.

He parked in front of Sam's Boots and walked inside to experience the same time-warp emotion as when he'd walked into
the Cora Café. The store also smelled the way he'd remembered:
leather and musty wool and polyester. A man in his late sixties
standing next to a hand-crank cash register behind the counter
asked if he could help.

"Is Sam here?" Justin asked.

The man's eyebrows furrowed.

"Sam's been gone this past 14 years. I'm his nephew. Store's
mine now."

"Sorry. I'm looking for some white shirts."

"All our shirts are over there, just past the boot section."

Justin looked at the boots, Tony Lamas, Ariats, Noconas
and Justins. He thought he should buy himself a pair of Justin
Boots just for the hell of it, but then thought better.

The shirts were displayed hanging from round metal racks
and in wall cubbies, winter wools mixed with summer cottons
and denims. There were Ropers, Cinches, PBRs, and George
Strait shirts, there were three Ariat shirts and he smiled — the
company was into vertical integration. But there were no white
dress shirts. Most had stupid snap buttons or shoulder yokes or
patterns, stripes and designs.

He glanced to see if Sam's nephew was watching and then
sniffed the fabric of several shirts, but the scents didn't make
him feel comfortable like the starched shirts his assistant bought

at Bergdorf Goodman. He could have her FedEx some shirts to him, but he wouldn't be staying that long.

He selected a denim shirt, tried it on and looked at himself in a full-length mirror. He looked like a hick. If any of his Manhattan associates saw him wearing it, he'd lose his credibility.

He bought four new shirts, put the denim one on and then stopped at the Cora Café for a cup of coffee. There was no one there to bother him and a waitress he hadn't seen before poured him a cup of coffee as though she'd had a bad morning.

He sipped the lukewarm brew and replayed the scene with Sara, knowing he should have behaved differently, but her words had been a shock. Then he thought about meeting Miss Adams. He hoped she didn't have anything dramatic to tell him. He'd had enough drama for one day.

As she'd promised, Miss Adams had left the front door unlocked. His voice echoed through stale air. He stood in the dim hall and listened to silence. As in his first visit, dust particles floated in sunbeams that sliced through cracks between curtains. A musky odor didn't seem right. He walked into the living room and saw her sitting doll-like in her favorite chair, her translucent face lit by the lamp. She stared at him with lifeless eyes.

He called her name. She didn't respond. He touched her face. Cold. No pulse in her carotid artery. He was too late. He looked at the withered corpse and remembered her vital energy, her enthusiasm and sensuality, but that was when she had been young. He was overwhelmed by sadness. She'd been responsible for his success. Tears ran down his cheeks.

A few minutes later, when he tried to close her eyelids, he smelled new odors — wilted flowers, rotting earth, talcum powder and urine. Her eyelids wouldn't stay shut. Her stare made him jittery.

He noticed the scholarship papers and a ballpoint pen lying on the table, the signature page on top. She'd signed the document. She'd removed from the table the photograph taken when she was in her thirties, and held it with one hand in her lap. The top edge of the leather frame leaned against her chest. The photo was image side out. She hadn't been looking at it; she'd wanted him to notice it.

He sat on the couch and stared at her, or what had been her. There was no vestige of her energy and he wondered where energy went when one died. Did it disappear into the ether? Was the spirit recycled into other forms? Did it die with the body? He wasn't certain that anyone knew. The faithful claimed to know, but where was the proof? Those questions were for the realm of religion or spirituality, and he didn't waste his time on belief without proof.

He walked through the house, into the bedroom where he and Cody had slept when storms forced them to stay in town. When they were young, she'd tucked blankets under their chins and her lilac scent would wash over him. He wandered into her bedroom, where he'd imagined . . . even now he felt guilty about his pubescent fantasies. He stood in the kitchen where she'd fussed over cooking them meals. And then he returned to the living room and still felt uneasy. Something wasn't right.

He looked at her again and decided she'd meant for him to have her photograph. He pried the picture frame from her fingers, picked up the scholarship papers, walked outside and put them on the front passenger seat of his car and then dialed 911.

An hour later, he stood on the sidewalk and watched men slide a stretcher containing Miss Adams' corpse into the back of the mortician's SUV, which substituted for the town's ambulance. One of the men told him that she'd made arrangements to be cremated. There would be no funeral. Her attorney would handle matters. Justin watched them drive off with his teacher's body and he felt a part of him leave with her.

First his old man had died, and now Miss Adams. They had influenced his life like negative and positive electrical charges.

He wondered what had happened to his mother. Now that his Dad and his teacher were gone, he was the oldest remaining member of his family. In the order of things, he was next. He touched his river stone and shuddered.

Chapter 22

Ugly clouds scuttled across mountaintops as Justin drove through the switchbacks toward Dead Man's Pass. Rain beat against the windshield. The wipers slapped back and forth in a dirge-like rhythm. Tires splashed through potholes, spraying muddy water. As he approached the spot where his old man had plunged off the road, he braked. The tires locked and the car skidded toward the edge. He eased off the brakes, straightened the wheels and stopped. He rolled down the foggy window to look at the cross. Raindrops splattered cold against his hand and wrist. The rain blurred his father's name. Mists swirled in the abyss below the drop off. Maybe, it had been an accident, he thought. But Cody had seen other tire tracks after their father had died.

He wondered what it had felt like — skidding off the cliff, plunging, tumbling for an eternity toward the ragged boulders. What had the old man thought about on his way down? In that split second before being crushed to death, had he heard the metal compress and shred? Had he seen sparks?

Suddenly it seemed everything was dying, even Cody's way of life. Justin sensed his own life would be changing. But he couldn't imagine the specifics. Perhaps even now something inside him was changing and he was being altered, from someone he knew well and could rely on, into someone much less familiar. The thought made him uneasy.

He drove toward the top of the pass. On the other side, the storm had blown through the valley. The landscape was clear and crisp, the forest vibrant green and the river that wove through the valley reflected silver. The valley looked different. It was a good earth.

He drove to Sara's. She wasn't at the barn, so he drove to her lodge. He took the picture of Miss Adams from the car, touched his river stone and then knocked on her door.

She opened the door.

"Sara. Look, I'm sorry. I wasn't prepared. It was a shock, and I acted like an ass."

"Yes, you did. But come in."

He followed her to the kitchen that smelled of baked bread and cinnamon. Copper pots and pans hung from iron hooks over a granite-topped island. He put the picture on a table in a nook surrounded by windows and then he sat down. Sunlight flooded the room and warmed him.

Sara brought a plate of hot cinnamon rolls, sat down and then poured coffee from a French press. She nodded at the picture. "You brought me a present?"

"My teacher gave me this — Miss Adams. It's a picture of her when she was young." He slid it across the table to her. She examined the photo.

"She was beautiful." Sara studied the picture. She looked up at him, looked at the picture again and then glanced up and held his eyes a moment.

"What?" he asked.

"Nothing." She handed him the picture.

"Age wasn't kind to her."

"Did you have a good visit?"

"She wanted to tell me something. When I got there, she was holding this in her lap."

"What did she say?"

His voice was hoarse. "She was dead."

"Oh, my God!"

He looked through the window at a hazy landscape. "It's been an emotional day."

"I'm so sorry."

"I was too late."

He told her about the visit and how Miss Adams had always been supportive, how he and Cody used to stay with her during storms and how she had saved his life by helping him get the scholarship to Harvard, so he could escape the ranch and his father's abuse. He told her about establishing the scholarship in Miss Adams' honor. He told her about sending Miss Adams a monthly check so she didn't have to go to the nursing home.

"Do you have any idea what she wanted to tell you?" Sara asked.

"I suppose she wanted to convince me that my dad quit drinking and changed for the better. She probably wanted to help me get over my anger. I'll never know."

"He did stop his drinking sometime after you left. And he did a lot of good in his later years," Sara said.

"So I'm told."

"Your dad gave Harry a lasso and taught him how to rope."

"Harry?"

"Harry spent his summers here and thought the world of your father."

"Oh." Outside, the tips of pine trees swayed in the breeze. "Does Harry know?"

She picked up her cup and drank some coffee. "Does it matter?"

"Of course it does."

She put the cup down, nodded and looked at him. "Harry knew Frank wasn't his father. He asked and I told him that I'd met a wonderful man, but we were too young to get married and that he'd left town before he knew I was pregnant and that I'd never heard from him again. Frank treated Harry as if he was his own. Frank was a terrific father and Harry loved him. Harry was never interested in his biological father."

"Did he know last night?"

"On the drive home, he told me how much he liked you, so I told him," she said.

Justin drank the last of his coffee and cleared his throat. "What now?"

"The next move is up to you. He'd like to hear from you, but that's your choice."

"I'd like to get to know him. When the time's right," he said.

"You mean, when you have time." Her voice held a sharp edge.

He looked at the pots and pans hanging above the stove and imagined her cooking for her husband and Harry. He wondered if those had been happy times with laughter and love.

He turned to her, "Why didn't you tell me you were pregnant?"

She put her elbows on the table and ran her fingers through her hair. "When you didn't answer my first two letters, I knew you weren't interested in continuing a relationship. Then I discovered I was pregnant. I thought about letting you know, but I thought you might drop out of Harvard and come to me. You would have missed your chance to get a great education. You'd fought so hard to escape your father and the ranch. You hated this valley. I knew you'd rejected everything about this place — your father, your brother, everything. We had a wonderful youthful affair, but I didn't know if we could love each other in a deeper way. I thought if you were forced to join me out of a sense of responsibility you'd grow to hate me, too. So I decided it would be better for all of us, including the baby, if you didn't know."

"You should have given me that choice," he said.

"Easy for you to say now."

"You could have gotten an abortion."

She leaned back in her chair and looked at the ceiling and then looked at him. "I thought about it. In the end, I wanted to have your baby."

A metal taste coated his mouth. He rose and walked to the sink and poured himself a glass of water. "I remember your parents were dead. How did you handle things?"

"I went back to Stanford that fall and then took the spring semester off. My grandparents were wonderful. I had Harry, went back to finish up school, met Frank. He was a professor. We were married and we lived in Palo Alto. My grandparents died and left me their estate and this place. So, on the whole, I've been lucky. I've been loved by a wonderful man, have a wonderful son and get to spend the best months of the year in my soul place. A person couldn't ask for anything more."

They sat in the silence of their own thoughts and then she stood up.

"Let's take a walk."

They walked under tall pines, footsteps cushioned by a carpet of needles, their bodies warmed by rays of the sun that slanted down through the canopy. They came to the edge of the forest and stood on a knoll that overlooked pastures and beyond the pastures, ancient cottonwood trees that lined the river and beyond that, mountains that rose to snow-covered peaks against a cobalt sky. High above, a bald eagle wheeled lazy circles, rising on the heat thermals, diving and rising and circling again without beating its wings.

"Every time I watch him, I imagine the joy of soaring. I wonder if he feels the same way?" she commented.

"I'd like to think so," he said and then he told her about the culture shock of Harvard and the East Coast, about meeting Ashley Farnsworth and even today not knowing if he'd been enamored by her wealth, her looks, or the opulent lifestyle. In fact, he didn't know if he'd ever really loved her. And he didn't know if she'd cared about him, or she'd wanted him because he was different from other men in her circles, a new plaything to mold into the man she imagined she wanted.

He talked about having Will and the crumbling of his relationship with Ashley and then the divorce. He told her about Ashley's new job that forced Will to live with him, and his fears that he wasn't certain he had been or could be a good father like Frank had been to Harry.

He told her about working for Ashley's father and about how, during the height of the dot com fever, he'd insisted that Farnsworth invest in the Pets.com startup. Farnsworth didn't believe in the Internet. Justin, caught in the excitement of the time, insisted the company would ride the wave into the future and be the best investment in the firm's history. He insisted they take a large position. Farnsworth reluctantly agreed, only if Justin would also make a major personal investment. Justin didn't have the money, so he borrowed a fortune from Farnsworth. Perhaps it was hubris or inexperience that made him agree to the usurious penalty that would have forced him into bankruptcy if not paid on the due date. The Pets.com investment was a fiasco — they lost everything. Justin faced bankruptcy and then he would have had to work forever for a man he'd grown to dislike. Thank God he'd had a terrific year and, with the last deal, he'd earned enough fees to pay off the loan and be free. And then he told her about Brad Duncan's incredible offer to join his firm and the freedom it would bring.

"Joining Duncan will make my dreams come true."

"I'm glad that makes you happy, Justin."

He looked at her and couldn't tell whether she was proud of his accomplishments or not. He didn't feel all that happy. He felt as though he'd missed something important in life, something impossible to regain.

Chapter 23

The next morning at the ranch, Justin called to check in with his assistant. She told him that Farnsworth was anxious to know when he would be returning. He told her that he'd be back as soon as he finished some estate details. Duncan had called. That was a good sign. He thought for a moment and then told her to tell Duncan that he'd call as soon as possible, but it might be a few days. He hung up and thought it would be good to let both men sweat a little.

After passing the shed on the way to the barn, he leaned against the corral and watched Cody and Will standing next to the dump truck. Will had the control box in his hand and Cody pointed out which way to move the joystick to raise and lower the truck's bed. Cody had become Will's hero. Justin felt envious.

A few minutes later, Cody suggested they all take a ride to inspect the far river pastures. Will saddled Baily and then Justin checked the rigging.

"Perfect. You're a fast learner," Justin said.

"This is a lot better than a stupid camp," he said.

"Not a reason to get suspended," Justin said.

Will gave him a look that he couldn't read. At least it wasn't accompanied by Ashley's tight-lipped smile.

Then Cody appeared at the door of the barn holding three

yellow slickers.

"Let's roll our slickers on the table in here."

Justin taught Will how to lay the slicker flat on the table, fold the arms into the front and then roll it tight to lash it behind the saddle.

Cody reached high above a rafter to retrieve a revolver in a leather holster.

"What's that for, Uncle Cody?"

"Never take a long ride without a pistol, a knife, a lighter and a slicker. The weather might change and you'll need the slicker to keep dry. You can use the lighter to start a fire to keep you warm and you need a knife if you need to cut or repair your saddle rigging."

"Why the pistol?" Will asked.

"You need it in case there's an accident and your horse breaks a leg. A horse can't recover from a broken leg," Cody said.

Will eyed the revolver.

"When shit hits the fan, you might have to put a horse down."

"Shoot it?"

"Hard to kill a horse with a knife. Come here and let me show you." Cody took the stainless steel revolver out of the holster.

"It's a Smith & Wesson .357 magnum. If it's okay with your Dad, we'll shoot it so you will be familiar with it."

"Can I, Dad?"

"I haven't seen that gun since I was a kid." He gave Cody a quick look. "I'll show you."

They walked a hundred yards from the barn, where Cody put two empty cans on top of fence posts. Justin showed Will how to open the cylinder and load cartridges.

"The cylinder holds six bullets, but you never want to put in more than five and always, always keep the hammer on the empty cylinder," Justin said.

"Why?"

"If the gun drops or there's an accident where the hammer gets hit, it will fall on the empty chamber. Otherwise, it could fire a cartridge and you could get hurt."

He showed Will how to hold the revolver in both hands, to pull back the hammer with his thumb, line up the front sight to fill the notch in the rear sight, put the sight at the bottom of the target, take a deep breath, partially exhale, and then slowly, slowly squeeze the trigger.

"Let me take the first shot, so you can watch."

He missed.

"Man, that's loud!" Will said.

Justin's second shot missed.

Cody grinned. "When was the last time you shot a gun?"

"When we went on our last elk hunt with the old man," Justin said.

"I remember that one. But, hey, once you ride a bicycle, you never forget." Cody said.

Justin's third shot blew a can off the fence post.

"You're right, it's just like riding a bike."

Justin reloaded.

"Can I try?" Will asked.

"I'll help you hold it so it won't kick so hard when it fires." Justin stepped behind his son and helped him hold the revolver at arm's length as the boy squeezed off a shot. It missed.

"What's that stink?" Will asked.

"Gun powder. Try again. Remember to keep your eyes open and squeeze the trigger slowly," Justin said.

The boy hit the can on his fourth shot. He handed the revolver to Justin and then whooped and did a celebration dance.

He'd never seen Will so excited. It was good to see the kid loosen up.

"Now it's your turn, Uncle Cody," Will said.

Cody reloaded the revolver and hit the can on his first try.

When they returned to the horses, Cody unhitched Baily from the post and handed Will the reins.

"Now listen close, Will, because I'm going to tell you how to put down a horse. No one likes to do it, but it's the most humane thing you can do. You have to put them out of their misery. You don't want to let your horse suffer. It's your responsibility to know where to put the bullet so death is instant.

"You draw an imaginary line from the base of the left ear to the right eye and then a line from the right ear to the left eye. Those two lines form an X. You want the bullet to go in right in the center of that X. The horse will usually let you put the muzzle of the gun close to his head, if you move slow, like this."

Cody slowly raised the revolver and pointed the muzzle inches from Baily's forehead. The horse didn't move. Will backed close to his father.

"Then you cock the hammer and, when the horse is still, pull the trigger. They fall dead faster than you can move, so don't get caught under them." Cody walked to his horse and put the revolver in his saddlebag.

"That's awful," Will said.

"No. It's kind to put them out of their misery," Justin said.

"Yeah, and it's high time you figured out how to put this ranch out of its misery," Cody said.

Justin squeezed his son's shoulder. "Let's mount up."

Will swung on Baily and nudged him with his heels. The horse threw his head down, crow-hopped, and then bucked. Will grabbed the saddle horn with his left hand and reined the horse's head tight toward his right knee. Baily spun in a fast circle. Will's hat fell off, trampled under the horse's hooves. After the fourth spin, the horse slowed and then finally stood still. Will looked at Cody and grinned.

"Looks like he's full of piss and vinegar today, Will. You did just like your Daddy taught you."

Will looked at Justin and nodded thanks. Cody picked up

the hat, punched it back into shape, wiped the dust off the brim and then handed it back to the boy.

"Starting to look like a real cowboy hat."

Justin winked and then untied the halter rope of his horse, Jake, from a corral post. He grasped the reins and a hank of Jake's mane in his left hand. He shortened the left rein, expecting the horse to shy away from him as he tried to mount. He hated putting his left foot in the stirrup and then having the horse skitter away, while he bounced along on his right toe, trying to get close enough to swing into the saddle. Only well-trained horses stood solid, and he couldn't remember any well-trained horses.

Jake stood rock solid as he put his left foot in the stirrup and swung his right leg over the saddle. The horse remained still while Justin settled into the seat. He turned to Cody, who sat the saddle on a bay gelding.

"I don't remember our old horses being solid. Jake's a good horse."

Cody grinned and tugged on his hat. "Yep. That Jake, he's a great horse. He likes you, Justin. You two belong together."

Later, at lunch, Linda informed them that Sara would be joining them for dinner.

"You call her or did she call you?" Justin asked.

"She said you left a picture with her and she wanted to return it, so I invited her for dinner. Why?" Linda asked.

"Just curious," Justin said.

After lunch, Justin returned to his cabin to call his investigator. The man's cigarette-hoarse voice said, "Found something interesting in your Cora banker's e-mails."

He'd discovered Kurt Kamm, the local banker who held the certificate of mortgage from the county's bankruptcy sale of the Thatcher ranch, planned to buy the mortgage the day after the redemption deadline and then flip the deed to Michael Gordon, a developer from Salt Lake City.

Gordon planned to turn the ranch into a world-class, exclusive and secure enclave for the super-rich, a place to flee and survive with other intellectual innovation leaders from future threats, a global economic meltdown, civil insurrections, biological or nuclear terrorism. There would be secure encrypted communications and bombproof vaults where owners could keep gold, cash, personal and corporate records.

"Gordon plans to cover his real purpose by making your ranch look like a recreational retreat with homes, a private ski hill, golf course, plus world class hunting and fishing.

"I checked out his premise. He's got a market. Rich people want to hang together. It's a tribal thing. I guess this guy figures a lot of them not only want to play together, but if push comes to shove, they'll want to survive together," the investigator said.

"How good is your information?" Justin asked.

"Their computer files and emails."

It continually amazed Justin how naive most business people were when it came to Internet privacy. "How much is Gordon paying the banker?"

"They have a non-binding contract for fifteen."

Justin hung up and repeated. "Fifteen million!"

This was his kind of deal. He'd get to Mike Gordon, who would have to protect his profits and offer him the same or better deal. He'd get a contract from Gordon, use it and the land as collateral for a loan to buy the redemption. Redeeming the mortgage would knock Kamm out of the deal, which would serve the greedy bastard right.

There'd be a minimum of thirteen million left after redeeming the ranch. That would give six-and-a-half-million each to Cody and him. Cody would have more than enough to find a better place, a ranch that could produce a good living. Justin would use his money to buy a larger equity piece in Duncan's firm to ensure that he'd be named the next chairman.

He called the developer, Mike Gordon. The man was traveling, so Justin made an appointment on the day after Gordon returned, which was close to the redemption deadline. This was turning out to be a great day!

That evening, Sara greeted Justin with graceful indifference as she handed him the photo of Miss Adams. Linda looked at the picture and then looked up at Justin with a strange expression and, when he asked what was wrong, she said "Nothing." He studied the picture and saw nothing unusual.

Will told Sara about Baily trying to buck him off. She clapped her hands together and laughed and told him how proud she was of him for learning from his father.

At the table, Justin watched her gossip and laugh with Cody and Linda about friends they'd visited with at the funeral. Everyone laughed at Cody's jokes. Justin wished he could make people laugh, but he simply didn't have the knack of spotting humor in situations, or telling stories, much less remembering them. He and Cody were different in so many ways.

Justin watched Sara's eyes sparkle. Her lips were quick to curve into smiles. Her hands moved with grace and liveliness as if they had a soul of their own. Those were the traits he'd been attracted to when they'd first met.

Sara acted as if he was not in the room, let alone sitting across the table from her. Under the table was another story. Her foot slid across his ankle and then disappeared. He stretched his leg and touched her foot. She moved it away.

Cody turned to him. "Figured out how to save our ranch?"

This wasn't the time to tell them about his conversation with his investigator. Once Cody realized how much money he'd get from the sale of the ranch and understood that he had an opportunity to buy another ranch that could throw off a profit, he'd be thrilled. "It'll work out."

"Not if it means I have to leave this place."

"What's so important about this place?" Justin asked.

"Because the land under our feet carries the stories that

make my life worth living."

"You're confusing that with memory. You can go anywhere and carry your stories with you. No one can take them away from you," Justin said.

"You don't get it, Justin. When you live on the land it speaks to you every day, every bit of it reminds you of stories, stories you could forget. Without living on this land my stories would fade and be forgotten."

"People leave all the time, our mother, for example."

Cody looked at Justin hard. He reached toward the floor for his plastic bottle and, without taking his eyes off Justin, spit tobacco juice into it. "That never bothered me like it did you."

"I don't believe that," Justin said.

"I remember when you left for out east, how pissed Dad was and how he threw horseshit against your back and shouted you wouldn't amount to shit."

Justin's jaw tensed. He felt Will's stare. Sara looked at her plate. Linda touched Cody's arm.

Cody moved his arm away and then he laughed. "And remember how you had me stop at Squaw Creek where you tried to wash the shit off your shirt? Left a brown stain, didn't it?"

"Let's talk about something else," Justin said.

"Well, look at you now. You sure proved Daddy wrong . . . at least from a money standpoint," Cody said with a sarcastic voice.

"Is that a compliment or criticism?"

"Any way you want to take it, brother."

They stared at each other. Neither blinked. Linda stood up and began clearing dishes. Will helped her. At the sink, Linda turned on the faucet to rinse the plates. The water spurted out a loud stream.

Sara turned to Cody. "I need to check the cows in the upper pastures tomorrow. Would you bring Will and help me?"

Will had been clearing the table, now he stopped, looked at

her and beamed.

Cody's eyes slowly turned to her and then grinned. "You bet. We'll be there first thing in the morning."

"I'll help, too," Justin said.

Sara shook her head. "Maybe some other time."

Chapter 24

The next morning, after Will and Cody gathered the horses, Justin told Cody that he would take Will to help Sara gather cows.

"She didn't want you," Cody said.

"Will is my son and I'm going to take him."

Cody shrugged. "Your poison."

Will watched them and remained silent.

Justin and Will hooked the trailer to the pickup, saddled Baily and Jake and then led their horses into the trailer. Will hopped in the passenger seat and Justin drove the rig toward Sara's.

Will finally broke the silence. "Sara doesn't want you to ride with us, Dad."

"I think you're right. Maybe she changed her mind. In any event, I want to ride with you."

They parked in front of the barn, where a saddled horse was tethered to a hitching post. They unloaded their horses. Sara walked out of the barn, stopped, put her hands on her hips and frowned at Justin.

"I thought we were clear that this was a two-man job," she said.

"We're two men," Justin said trying to sound humorous.

She shook her head.

"I'd like Dad to come."

Sara looked at the boy and then smiled. "If that's what you want, but he rides drag."

"Huh?"

"That means I get to ride in back of the cattle and get to eat dust," Justin said.

"That'll be neat," Will said.

They mounted up and rode through a pasture, stopped to open a boundary fence gate and then they followed a game trail under a brilliant sky. The morning sun painted distant limestone cliffs blood red and Justin inhaled the pungent scent of sagebrush. All seemed right with the world, except he couldn't figure out why Sara had a burr under her saddle . . . or as they said in Manhattan, why she had PMS.

The trail wove through a small meadow that contained a bubbling spring that made a gentle popping sound. They were soon enveloped by fragrant scents. The meadow was a carpet of spring flowers: blue lupine, snow buttercups, purple shooting stars and white spring beauties.

He took the lead as they rode through the flowers and then the trail penetrated a thick forest where a jumble of downfall cut visibility to a few yards. He hated dark places like this.

There was an explosion of breaking branches. A bull moose crashed through the timber onto the trail and spun to face them. Its massive horns were covered in velvet. The breath from its bulbous nose formed white vapor clouds in the shadows.

Jake's ears snapped forward and his muscles quivered, but he remained solid. The other horses snorted. Sara's horse reared and spun in an attempt to flee. She regained control. The moose turned, trotted thirty yards down the trail, veered left and then burst through downed timber until they could no longer hear the crashing.

"That was exciting!" Will said.

"Wasn't that the first moose you've seen?" he asked.

"Yeah. Cool!"

At noon, they watered their horses at a creek and then Justin tied the horses to a high-line he strung with his lariat between two trees so the horse's hoofs wouldn't damage the roots. They pulled sack lunches from their saddlebags. Justin found a comfortable place to sit under a pine tree. Sara asked Will to follow her. Justin was about to follow. She shot him a warning look. He shrugged. He'd gotten this far over her objections. Time to let her win one.

She hopped across the tops of exposed boulders to the other side of the creek. Will made it without falling in. Justin leaned against the tree trunk, ate his sandwich and watched them talk and laugh.

It appeared that Sara was asking Will questions. The boy responded with unusual cheerfulness. Their laughter rose over the sound of the creek. One time, they looked at him and laughed again. Another time, they shot him dark looks.

Later, he watched them skip back across the tops of creek boulders. He stood to greet them and asked what they'd been talking about.

Will looked at Sara with a guilty look. "Just stuff."

"Just stuff," she agreed.

"If I didn't know better, I'd think you two have been plotting against me."

"Don't you wish?" Her eyes held a mischievous sparkle.

She touched Will. "You're it."

"Huh?" The boy looked perplexed.

Justin had a terrible thought — he didn't know his son well enough to know if the boy had ever played tag. "You know what to do?"

"Like, yeah," Will said and touched Sara. "You're it!"

They ran and Sara chased them through wildflowers and around tree trunks. She tagged Will. "We're both 'it'. Let's get your Dad."

They cornered him at the edge of the creek, so he hopped across boulders toward the other side. A rock shifted. His arms flailed and then he fell into ice-cold water. They dropped to their knees laughing and then helped him out. He hung his shirt over a bush to dry and sat in the sun to warm.

Later, they mounted up and followed Sara to a far meadow and gathered the cows and calves and then began pushing them down dusty trails toward large corrals near the barn. He watched Will follow Sara's instructions without hesitation.

Will didn't complain about the dust, which covered him like shrink-wrap. Sara taught the boy how to tie a bandana over his nose and mouth, and he laughed when she told him he looked like a bandit.

Will handled his horse like a natural. Justin couldn't believe the boy had only had several days riding experience. On the other hand, Baily had years of experience with kids and cattle. You didn't need to have experience if you rode a horse like Baily.

Justin marveled at how well Jake behaved. He was becoming fond of the damned horse.

Later, while the cattle paused to drink from a stream, they rode to a bare knob that overlooked the mountains. Justin pointed to a distant promontory that jutted out from the cliffs.

"Remember our vision quest spot, Sara?"

"What's that?" Will asked.

"It's a sacred place where young Indians went alone for a quest in the wilderness. They thought it was a spot to go to find themselves and discover their intended spiritual life direction."

"How do you know about it?" Will asked.

"We found it when we were young," Sara said.

"So did you find yourselves?" Will asked.

"You might say that," Justin said.

Sara blushed.

Will looked at them both and then grinned.

"A young Indian would sit inside the circle without shelter, food or water, until he saw a vision. Sometimes it took days. They often took their adult names from what they witnessed, like Spotted Wolf, or Leaping Deer or something like that."

"Like Pooping Bear?" Will asked.

They laughed.

"Why did they go there alone?" Will asked.

"That's part of the tradition," Justin said.

"Do you ever feel alone, Dad?" Will asked.

Justin was startled by the question. He looked at Sara. She raised her eyebrows.

"Everyone feels alone sometimes."

He leaned his forearms on the saddle horn. He'd always felt alone. Always felt different from others. Couldn't remember when the feeling started. Maybe he'd been born feeling alone. Maybe the feeling started when his mother disappeared. All he knew for certain was that he'd always felt alone since he'd left the ranch.

"Do you feel lonely?" Justin asked.

"Yeah, sometimes. Like at school I feel different and alone and I feel sad when I think about it."

"But you're having a good time now, right?" Sara asked.

Will nodded.

After a beat, Justin changed the subject. "George Horse Capture, who used to be the curator at the Plains Indian Museum in Cody, said certain vision quest sites were unique spots on earth that focused special powers beyond human understanding."

"I don't get it," Will said.

"Lots of things happen that don't make sense. Like the visions Indians had — talking with their ancestors or with animals or other strange spirits," Justin said.

"Did that happen to you?" Will asked.

"No. I don't have the imagination for those sorts of things to happen. I'm not a woo-woo sort of a guy," he said. And then he remembered his nightmare bear.

Chapter 25

By late afternoon, they'd corralled the cattle and had un-saddled and brushed the horses.

"Thanks for your help, Will," Sara said. "You handled your-self well. You should be proud of yourself."

The boy grinned. "What do you think, Dad?"

"I agree. I couldn't have done as well when I was your age."

Sara invited them to stay for dinner. They walked up the drive through aspen trees and over a stone bridge that spanned a small creek, toward her log home that nestled under pines on top of a bluff. In the kitchen, she fixed them iced tea.

"Get cleaned up and I'll start dinner."

"Great!" Will said.

"We'd love to, but I've got to get back," Justin said.

"Why?" Sara asked.

"I need a clean shirt."

A troubled look crossed Sara's face. She held up a fin-ger for them to wait and then walked out of the room. Sev-eral minutes later she returned with a man's shirt and blue jeans.

He looked at them and then at her. "You sure?"

She nodded. "By the way, there was a message. Ed High-street wants you to call as soon as possible."

He called the attorney, listened and then agreed to drive

into Cora to meet first thing in the morning. He hung up.

"He needs to talk with me about Miss Adams."

"What about?"

"He wouldn't tell me."

Sara led them to Harry's bedroom. Will looked through Harry's books while Justin showered.

He put on the clean shirt and pants Sara had given him. It felt weird to wear her dead husband's clothes. Will got into the shower and Justin wandered toward the family room. Framed pictures lined the hall, photos that depicted Sara's life: her wedding with Frank, baby Harry, Harry with his first pony, with horses, herding cattle, pack trips, fishing, hiking, picnics, dances, parties, and then Sara and Frank with Harry at his graduation. There were no more pictures. Justin assumed she'd stopped putting photos up after Frank's death.

He felt like a voyeur looking into an intimate life that he'd never imagined. That could have been his life, if he'd responded to her letters. Maybe. But even that wasn't as weird as wearing her husband's clothes.

"Looking at my life?"

He startled. "Wonderful pictures."

She touched the sleeve of his shirt and then looked at the pictures. "It was a good life," she said.

"It's not over, Sara."

"I didn't mean it that way," she said with a brittle voice. She led him back to the kitchen where she had made sandwiches. Will joined them, famished.

After dinner, he lit a fire in the fireplace. Sara pulled out a thin volume from a bookcase.

"We always read to Harry after dinner. Why don't you read to us?" She handed the book to Justin.

They sat on the couch and he began to read Jack London's *To Build a Fire.* Sara draped her arm over Will's shoulder. Her fingers touched Justin's hair.

He faltered.

"What's wrong, Dad?"

"Nothing." He cleared his throat and continued reading. He felt the warmth of the fire and the brush of Sara's fingers on the back of his neck.

After finishing the story, he said, "We'd better head back."

"It's late. You could spend the night here," Sara suggested.

"Can we, Dad?"

He liked the idea of spending the night with Sara, bodies entwined, the smell of her breath, the touch of her body and later they'd sleep cupped together under a down blanket . . . if it weren't for Will. More likely her invitation was simply a good-hearted gesture. "We'll take a rain check."

They stood on the porch and Sara hugged Will and kissed his cheek. "Thanks for your help today, Will. I had fun."

"Me too."

They watched Will turn and walk toward the barn.

"Would you come to town with me tomorrow?" Justin asked her.

"Why?" Sara asked.

"I don't know. I have a funny feeling about meeting with Highstreet. He sounded strange. I don't want to be alone. I'll be driving past your place at seven."

"I could pick up some groceries while you meet with him."

He put his arms around her and bent to kiss her lips. She gently pushed him away and told him she'd be ready to go in the morning.

Driving home, Will turned as if to say something, but then looked out the passenger side window.

"What?" Justin asked.

"You wanted to kiss her?"

"Maybe."

"What about Mom?"

"Your mother doesn't like me. I thought you liked Sara."

"I do, but . . ."

Several minutes later, Will turned toward him again.

"Uncle Cody told me I could stay here as long as I want."

"That's not possible. Don't be ridiculous."

Will crossed his arms and looked out the side window.

"I won't go back. No matter what you do or say, I won't go back!"

Chapter 26

The next morning, Justin picked up Sara and drove toward Cora. They chatted about the ride yesterday and then moved on to when they'd discovered the vision quest place, their words skirting around their love-making within the sacred circle. He remembered the heat of the sun, the sheen of sweat glistening on their naked bodies, the smell of her breath and the embrace of her arms. And he remembered that he had hoped that moment would last forever. They drove over Dead Man's Pass in the comfortable silence of private memories.

Later, when he parked in front of Ed Highstreet's office, she said she'd wait in the car.

"Thought you needed groceries."

"I lied."

"Come in with me."

"I don't mind waiting."

"I need you."

Inside Highstreet's office, Justin began to introduce her.

Sara cut him off. "Ed and I are old friends. He's my local attorney."

"So what's this about?" Justin asked.

"You are the sole beneficiary of Miss Adams' estate. She told me you would know what best to do with the money."

"What money?" Justin asked.

"She left you well over a million dollars of U.S. Treasury bonds, plus her house and furnishings, minus expenses."

"That's impossible!" Justin said.

"Her parents left her money. And, as you remember, she lived a modest lifestyle," the attorney said.

Justin leaned back and stared at the cheap print of the cowboys in yellow slickers. A million? Unbelievable. He'd never asked if she needed money. He'd assumed it. All together he'd kicked in about a hundred-fifty thousand. And she kept thanking him and telling him he was keeping her out of the county nursing home. Be damned!

"When's the funeral?" Sara asked.

"She was quite firm about having no funeral. She's here," Highstreet pointed to a black box on the edge of his desk. "She wants you to spread her ashes according to the instructions in this letter." He handed Justin a sealed envelope with his name written in her meticulous handwriting.

"There's just one more thing."

Highstreet handed Justin a cheap photo album with a black cardboard cover. And then the attorney walked him through the details of settling the estate.

They left Highstreet's office, put Miss Adam's envelope, photo album and her remains between them on the front seat and drove to the Cora Café. They took a booth in back, ordered coffee. He put the photo album and envelope on the table. The waitress arrived with coffee and chatted with Sara about a sick friend. When she walked back to the kitchen, Sara asked if he was going to open the envelope.

He looked at the envelope and shook his head. "Come over and sit next to me. Let's look at the pictures first."

Sara slid in next to him, pushed their coffee cups out of the way and waited for him to open the album. He wasn't sure he wanted to know what was inside, but he touched his river stone and pressed on. The first picture was of a newborn baby that looked vaguely familiar. That was a surprise; he'd expected a picture of Miss Adams. There was no writing to identify the baby. He turned the page. There was a naked baby boy sitting on a woman's lap. The woman's image had been scissored out. He recognized the picture and the woman's hand holding the baby.

Heaviness pressed against his chest as he flipped the next page. The boy was standing now, his hand held by a woman whose image had been sliced out.

He felt Sara's left hand touch his arm.

Every page held a picture of the boy, growing older, with the background and people scissored out. There was a picture of Miss Adams and the boy taken at his high school graduation. Justin's mother, who had stood on his left while his father took the picture, had been cut out of the photo.

"Can't be!" Sara said

He said nothing. He turned other pages. Near the end of the album, there was a wedding photo, the picture he'd sent her.

Ashley's image had been hacked out.

He turned the last page to find the only complete image in the album, a picture of Justin holding baby William.

"This is creepy," he said.

He picked up the envelope. "We might as well get this over with." He inserted a finger under the flap and tore it open and took out a handwritten letter:

My dear Justin,

By the time you read this, you'll know how much I loved you. My only regret is that I didn't have more time with you, but our brief times together were wonderful. Thank you for everything you did to make my life as good as it could have been, under the circumstances.

I'd like you to scatter my ashes where this map shows. Scatter them on a beautiful day in the late afternoon. You'll understand.

Love,

The letter was unsigned.

He imagined Miss Adams sitting at her desk, pen in hand, unable to sign the truth.

There was nothing more. No explanation, no reason, no answer to the questions that would help make sense of this.

"What now?" Sara asked.

"She wanted her ashes to be scattered on a beautiful afternoon. It's a beautiful afternoon."

They followed the map twenty-three miles up the Middle Fork River, swung left on a Forest Service gravel road for three miles to the parking area for Beauty Lake. Following the map, they walked half way around the lake, climbed a bluff that overlooked deep blue waters that reflected snowcapped mountains. They stopped and stood on a soft bed of pine needles under the huge tree marked on Miss Adams' map. The sun was low, the light soft.

"What a romantic place," Sara said.

He gave her a sharp look.

"Sorry. But it is wonderful."

They stood for a few minutes before he pried off the lid of the black plastic box and shook out some of the ashes. He snapped the lid back on the box.

"You didn't scatter all of her," she said.

"Enough to make her happy." He didn't know what to call her.

They drove in silence back through town toward Dead Man's Pass.

"Want to talk about it?" she asked.

"No."

"Those nights when you stayed with her. Did she ever touch you?"

"It was never like that." Justin paused. "I need time to think about this before I tell Cody and Linda."

"I won't say anything." She reached for his hand.

On the pass, he drove past the white cross and realized his old man had had a secret life behind the one he knew, and maybe even one behind that. Perhaps that was why he had intuitively never trusted or liked him. His father had lived a different life after Justin had left and a secret life while he was there. Justin wondered if everyone was like that. Maybe that explained his instinct to trust no one.

When they pulled into her ranch, Sara asked, "Do you want to spend the night?"

"I need to be alone to think."

"Call if you need me, even if it's in the middle of the night." She kissed him on the cheek and said goodbye.

Will was in their cabin, sitting in the Lazy-Z-Boy and playing his video game.

"What did you and Sara do in town?"

He told the boy that they had met with the attorney who told him he was executor of Miss Adam's estate. Will asked what "executor" and "estate" meant. He explained that he had to sell her house and pay her bills and close her bank accounts. Will seemed to listen closely.

"So that means we're going to be staying here longer?"

He shook his head. "We'll have to see."

After Will went to bed, Justin walked outside. The shed was a grotesque shadow against a black night. He sat in the rocking chair and thought about the day. Maybe he was interpreting the photo album wrong. Maybe Miss Adams had been unable to have children and developed a sick need to have a surrogate son. Maybe, after he left the ranch, his father had given her the pictures.

And what was the meaning of spreading her ashes at that particular spot? His thoughts bounced back and forth like balls at a Chinese ping-pong match. And always returned to the weird scissoring of everyone's image. He shivered and then walked to the car to retrieve the black box containing the remainder of

Miss Adams' ashes. He went inside and opened the lid to the Folgers can that contained his old man's ashes and mixed them together. He sat in his father's chair and stared at the coffee can that contained the ashes of his mother and his father.

Chapter 27

Something touched Justin's shoulder. He tried to open his eyes, but they were stuck together and his mind slid back down into a dark place. Something shook him hard. He cracked opened his eyes. An image was out-of-focus. Then he recognized Will. The boy looked frightened. Justin had fallen asleep in the Lazy-Z-Boy. He imagined how he might look and assured his son he was okay — he'd just fallen asleep. Will looked at him with concern and then turned and walked out the door to go to breakfast.

A few minutes later, Justin called Sara.

"The other day, when I stopped by after Miss Adams died and you looked at her picture? Why did you give me a strange look?" he asked.

"Would you like me to come over?" she asked.

"No. What did you see?"

"I'm not sure I saw anything."

"You noticed something," he said.

After a pause, she said, "You might want to hold her picture next to your face and look in the mirror."

He hung up, walked into the bedroom, picked up the photograph and looked into the mirror. He immediately saw what Sara had noticed — it was in the eyes. His eyes were a spitting image of hers.

He walked back into the bedroom and compared the photo of Miss Adams to the photo his old man had taken of his mother. They were identical — the same pose of the women, the same silhouette of his father with the shadow of his Stetson covering the same part of their bodies.

He slammed the pictures on top of the dresser. Glass shattered on one or both. He didn't give a damn. He walked outside and sat in the rocker and looked at the shed. A shadow from a cloud darkened it, and then, as the cloud moved, the shed brightened again, giving him the sensation that it was breathing. Waiting for him.

His fists clenched. He was slipping over the edge. No, he wasn't teetering on the edge — he'd been pushed off.

He imagined different scenarios — his old man bringing the baby home, lying to his mother. No, not his mother. If not, what was she? His stepmother? His old man's wife? Did the bastard beat her into submission to raise him as her son? Or was it her idea? Had she ever loved him? He'd never know, but now he felt certain that he'd been the cause of her disappearance. But why did she wait eleven years?

He walked along the riverbank toward Cody's cabin. Otto sat on the porch watching him. As Justin approached the dog growled and then laid down and let him pass without threatening him. Even the dog thought he was different.

Will and Cody sat at the kitchen table finishing eggs and bacon. Linda was not there. He heard the shower running. He poured a cup of coffee and then leaned against the kitchen counter and looked at his brother.

"Thought you would have torn down the shed by now," Justin said.

"Figured you'd come back some day, so I saved it for you," Cody said.

Pretending not to hear their exchange, Will mopped up the yellow egg yolk with a piece of toast.

Cody was full of bullshit. Maybe Cody left the shed as some sort of sick memorial, a reminder that Cody had been the old man's favorite. Maybe Cody wanted to leave it standing to torment him, if he ever returned. Maybe Cody did save it for him, so he could confront his memories.

Hell, he couldn't figure out his brother. Perhaps Cody was telling the truth, but nothing here was as it seemed. His brother appeared straightforward and honest, and yet he couldn't be certain, because they were so damned different. At least he now knew why — they were only half brothers.

"Is there a sledge hammer around here?" Justin asked.

"Yeah, and a crow bar," Cody said, and then he turned to Will.

"Your Dad's gonna be busy this morning. I need you to help me with some chores down at the barn."

Will shrugged and shoved his boots on and followed Cody out the door.

Justin found a nine-pound sledgehammer and a long handled crowbar and then he walked to the homestead cabin, climbed to the porch, turned and gazed at the shed, the door now closed.

He remembered the day he had left the ranch. His brother had been behind the wheel of Old Tan, waiting to drive him to the bus stop. He'd packed his belongings in a cardboard suitcase — a spare pair of jeans, one clean shirt, two boxer shorts and socks — and he walked out of the cabin toward the truck. His old man stood between the cabin and Old Tan, raking up horse manure. Justin brushed past without speaking — there was nothing left to say. Close to the truck, he heard running footsteps from behind. He forced himself not to turn around. His father threw wet manure on his back. It shoved Justin forward with a soft thudding sound and stuck to his shirt, and then slid down and finally fell to the ground. His dad screamed, "Go to that goddamned fancy college, but you'll never amount to nothing! You ain't nothing but a piece of shit!"

Justin threw the suitcase in the bed of the truck and then he stripped off the wet shirt and tossed it in back. He didn't look at his father or wave goodbye or give him the finger, like he wanted to. He wouldn't acknowledge the old man or his words, but those words cut deep.

He had Cody stop at Squaw Creek, where he rinsed out the shirt and had his brother splash water on his back before wiping it clean with an old rag. He put on his clean shirt for the trip out east. After he arrived in Cambridge, he washed the shirt many times, but it was permanently stained. He'd given the shirt to a homeless man, who looked at it and then tossed it into a trash can.

He walked down the stairs, turned toward the shed and began counting steps out loud — one, two, three . . . at thirty-three he stopped, dropped the tools, opened the door and stared inside the empty shed.

He saw vivid scenes — his mom's hand frantically rubbing condensation from the kitchen window. Her face mirrored in the circle, helpless eyes peering out, looking at him as he walked past. Shaking her head. Covering her eyes. The flare of a match his old man used to light the Coleman lantern hanging from a beam. The shadows. Spiders crawled away from the light, scurrying for the cracks in the wood, hiding, with parts of their grotesque bodies and legs visible. The leather belt swung gently from his old man's fist.

Justin slammed the door shut. He rammed the wooden latch home to lock inside the screams and pain.

He picked up the sledgehammer, walked to the back of the structure and studied the wall for its weakest spot. He raised the sledgehammer over his right shoulder like a baseball bat. He screamed and then swung with a lifetime of anger. The rusted steel head exploded through shattered wood, its momentum propelling it inside. He held on to the shaft, lost his balance and fell against the splintered wall. He ripped his shirt and tore his skin bloody. He pushed away, extracted the sledgehammer and swung at the walls with a cleansing fury. He demolished the back wall, board by board, until it lay in ruins. Gasping for breath, he sat on the ground for rest. Later, he rose and destroyed the side-wall with the same vehemence.

His hands throbbed, shirt wet with sweat and his lungs screamed for oxygen, but he kept pounding the shed.

He destroyed part of the far wall and then felt dizzy. He dropped the sledgehammer and fell to his hands and knees. Chest heaving, he gasped for breath. He gagged and then vomited. When the dry heaves quit, he looked at blisters on his hands. He should have worn gloves — too late now.

He rose, unsteady, and raised the sledgehammer over his head, and then flailed at the remaining wall until only the door, roof and corner posts remained. He rested again. His chest hurt and he felt sleepy. He wondered if he was going to have a heart attack. If he did, so be it. It wouldn't matter.

Sometime later, he staggered to the front of the shed and paused, catching his breath. A thought flitted through his mind — he could simply open the damned door and use the crowbar to pry off the hinges. Fuck it! He would never again open that door.

He brought the sledgehammer down against the door again and again until it lay shattered in the rubble. The shed was now gone, except for the four corner posts holding up the roof. His first blow snapped a post in half. The roof swayed, but did not fall. He stumbled through the debris and smashed the opposite post. The roof tottered, but again refused to fall. He lurched to the third post and smashed it. The last remaining post snapped and the roof crashed down on top of the wreckage.

He dropped the sledgehammer and sank to his knees. He

didn't know how long it had taken to destroy the shed, or how long he had been on his knees, but it was over now and that was good. Later, he'd get the tractor with its front-end bucket and clear the debris into the dump truck and then haul them to a pit and burn them. Now it was time to wash up.

Until now, he had moved on with his life as if nothing had happened. That's the way it had been in the old days, after the old man took him to the shed. His mother pretended nothing had happened. She never protected him. She refused to talk about it. No one talked about it, not his old man, not Cody, not him. Life and the beatings went on. Now it was finished. He hoped.

Chapter 28

When Justin emerged from the cabin, washed and wearing a clean cowboy shirt, he saw Cody and Will walking across the yard. They stopped to examine what was left of the shed. Cody grinned. "Well, you sure knocked the shit outta that."

Justin nodded. That said, that was all that needed saying.

"Linda and I are leaving for the annual horse auction in Missoula on Friday. Be gone the weekend. Want to join us?" Cody said.

"Can I go, Dad?"

"Sure, but I'll pass. I want to stick around. Sara and I've planned a ride," Justin said.

That afternoon Justin and Will walked to the barn. The boy sat in his lap and drove the tractor to the demolished shed. Cody brought the dump truck.

"I've got some fencing to do in the lower pasture. You don't need me to clean up that mess."

Justin taught Will how to use the bucket to lift debris and drop the broken boards into the bed of the dump truck, and then he let Will drive the truck to the burn pit, but there he took over because Cody had piled a number of huge limestone slabs to use as rip-rap to stop river bank erosion and it would be difficult for Will to back the truck to the edge of the pit. He put the truck in park, left the engine running and then stood next to the passenger side door where Will held the control box to raise the bed. The boy moved the joystick, but nothing happened.

"You're holding the box upside down. Turn it around and try again."

Will turned the control box around and moved the joystick and the bed rose faster than he'd imagined and the rubble slid into the pit. They drove back and took a twenty-foot logging chain from behind the truck's front seat, tied it around the stump of one of the shed's corner posts, hooked it to the tractor's bucket and yanked each post from deep in the ground. They trucked the remainder of the wreckage to the pit. He found a bucket of saw dust and diesel fuel starter in the barn. Will scattered the mixture over the remains of the shed, and then struck and lobbed matches into the wreckage. They watched together, silent, while flames consumed the remains of the damned shed. Black smoke poisoned a blue sky.

Will glanced at him. "Feel better?"

He looked at his son and wondered how much he knew. "Cody tell you about the shed?"

"Yeah. He said you hated it and always wanted to tear it down."

"That is true," he agreed.

And that was all that needed to be said for now, but he'd be happy to tell the boy more, if he asked and when the time seemed right

Later that afternoon, Justin gathered Frank's clothes and drove to Sara's. His hands were painful, so he drove with his wrists. She opened the front door.

"You look tired," she said.

"I'm okay."

"What happened to your hands?"

"I forgot to wear gloves when I tore down the shed."

"So it's gone?" she said.

"Yes."

"Is it done?"

"I hope so." He handed her the shirt and pants she'd loaned him. He followed her inside and watched her put them on top of a stack of a man's clothes piled on the floor.

She turned to him, her smile melancholy. "I'm cleaning out Frank's closet."

"Oh."

"Are you all right? I mean about yesterday. I'll make some coffee if you'd like to talk," she said without enthusiasm.

"No, I have to get back to pack. I'm leaving in the morning," he said.

Her eyes widened. "Leaving?"

"On business. Just for a day, maybe a day and a half."

"Oh. Then I'll see you when you get back."

"You won't be able to keep me away." Justin kissed her on the cheek and then drove back to the ranch.

At dinner Justin announced he had to leave for a short trip. He might be gone for several days.

Will didn't seem to be disappointed.

Cody asked why.

"I have some business," Justin said.

"About the ranch?" Cody asked.

"Other things."

Later, after Will had gone to bed, he walked upstairs and sat on his old bed and looked at his son.

Will peered at him from under the blanket. "What?"

"I'm leaving in the morning . . ."

The boy cut him off. "I know that already. Why did you come up here?"

Justin looked at the grille he and Cody used to stand on when they dressed on cold winter mornings.

He cleared his throat. "I just wanted ... I just wanted to say goodnight."

Chapter 29

In Missoula early the next morning, Justin's jet roared off the runway for Salt Lake City. His research indicated Mike Gordon was one of the leading contributors to the Mormon Church, with the reputation of being hard working and honest in his business dealings with fellow Mormons. There were rumors about his dealings with those outside the faith, but gossip shadowed most successful businessmen. Best part was that Mike Gordon was said to be a bottom-line guy, and Justin knew how to work with that kind.

The Gordon Development Company's office was a prefabricated metal building reflecting a style some called Mormon Efficient. The reception area held used furniture and the ceiling tiles were yellowed with age, but the place was spotless.

Justin patted his river stone as the receptionist walked him down a narrow hall to a large office. Gordon sat behind a metal desk. He rose and walked around the desk to greet Justin with a firm handshake. Gordon was a tall, thin man with ape-like arms and a head of unruly black hair. He had sincere black eyes.

"What can I do for you, Mr. Thatcher?"

"Hear you're interested in buying our family ranch."

"I'm sorry, don't remember having discussed . . ."

"You have a non-binding contract with Kurt Kamm to buy it as soon as the redemption period is over."

His eyebrows arched. "Who gave you that story?"

"Let's not dance around the facts, Mr. Gordon. I'm going to redeem the property. Kamm will not gain title, so you're going to buy it from me for twenty million."

"It's not worth that much," Gordon said.

"Your option contract with Kamm is for fifteen million. For what you're planning, it's worth more than twenty."

"How the devil . . ."

"I'm redeeming the title and I'm considering other options for the property. If I hadn't heard about your deal with Kamm, I would have signed another deal."

Gordon's eyebrows furrowed. "He told me you were a big city hot-shot."

"And if you've checked my reputation, you'll know once I set a deadline and make a decision, I never change my mind."

"I have a banker in New York. He told me about your reputation."

"You have plans for our ranch that will tap into an extremely profitable market. Our property is unique. Buying it eliminates the risks of fighting government bureaucracies, environmental hotheads and lawsuits. I need a decision now, Mr. Gordon. Yes or no?"

"I don't like to be pressured."

"I don't like being distracted. I need your decision."

"I'll think about it and let you know."

"Think fast, because I will not deal with you after I walk out of this office," he said.

"You're full of bull, Mr. Thatcher. Maybe, just maybe, given a couple years and a hot stock market, you could find a buyer who'd cough up ten million for your place. You're too good of a businessman to walk out of here and leave five on the table."

"Five million is nothing. I can make that up in one morning's work."

"Sixteen. Not a penny more," Gordon said.

"You're at sixteen. I'm at twenty. Split the difference," Justin said.

"Eighteen's too steep. I can't make a profit. Sixteen is my top dollar."

"I've learned that it's foolish to walk away from a unique deal for a couple of million. Our ranch is unique. Once it's gone, it's gone forever. You'll make a killing when you pay twenty million and you know it. The price is eighteen."

"It looks like we're at an impasse, Mr. Thatcher."

"We're not at an impasse. You just told me you're not going to buy our ranch. Thank you for your time." Justin rose and walked toward the door.

"Wait!" Gordon's voice was hoarse.

He turned.

Gordon stood behind his desk, face red, hands balled into fists.

"All right. Eighteen, but not one damned penny more."

Justin sat down. Now was the time to let the man save face.

"We have a deal. Now let me propose a plan to reduce the price back to your original offer of sixteen. It will save you two million."

Gordon's eyebrows arched. "I'm listening."

Justin outlined his plan.

Gordon nodded. "You've got a deal. Maybe you aren't as big a bastard as everyone says."

After they signed a letter of intent, Gordon walked him to the door and then shook hands.

"Watch yourself between now and the time you redeem your mortgage, Mr. Thatcher."

"Why?"

"My contract with Kurt Kamm is still in place. He'll lose millions if you redeem the mortgage. That's a lot of money."

On the drive back to the airport, Justin found a ranch supply shop and bought a lariat made by King Ropes of Sheridan, Wyoming. A half-hour later, he climbed into his jet, buckled into his seat and looked out the window at the Mormon Temple and the Wasatch Mountain Range that dominated Salt Lake City's skyline. He imagined Gordon was now on the phone talking with Kurt Kamm, re-negotiating their previous deal. Gordon would win either way. What would Kamm do to save his millions?

He flew to Billings for a meeting with the region's leading ranch real estate and mortgage company. He pledged the ranch for a bridge loan to redeem the mortgage before Monday's deadline.

The money would be wire transferred to his Manhattan bank account. Justin's personal banker would FedEx Ed Highstreet a cashier's check for the exact amount owed. Justin would meet Highstreet at his office Monday morning, the redemption deadline, to pick up the check, and then to go to the courthouse to redeem the mortgage.

Dick Gordon's attorneys would send Highstreet the contract for the sale of the ranch signed by Gordon, who would not be able to back out of the deal. As soon as Justin redeemed the mortgage, he'd sign the Gordon contract and that would seal the transaction.

Flying back to Missoula, Justin looked out the window at the tops of scattered clouds. It had been a good day, a very good day. The insecurities created by Miss Adams death, the mysteries about his roots, and the threatened sense of self, really didn't matter in the world he'd reentered after leaving the ranch. Today's negotiations with Gordon had confirmed who he was — a world-class businessman. Going back to his old man's funeral and all that had happened there were parts of his past, a past he'd buried once and would bury again next week after he redeemed the ranch, flipped it, and then returned to Manhattan. He could bury it all, except Sara. He would take her with him to share his future.

He called his assistant and told her he would be returning to Manhattan in the middle of next week.

Chapter 30

That afternoon, on the drive from Missoula to Cora, Justin called the ranch to talk with Will. Linda said the boy was at Sara's. He called her and left a message that he'd stop and pick him up on his way.

Herds of elk and deer fed on the slopes leading to Dead Man's Pass. A golden eagle soared above red cliffs. He stopped at the cross that memorialized his father's accident and smiled. He'd amounted to more than shit and he'd just proved it.

"You were wrong, old man."

He parked near the barn where Sara and Will were raking horse manure from an outside stall. She leaned her rake against the rails as he stepped out of the car.

"Welcome back!" Sara said.

The boy took off his Stetson and rubbed his head. His hair had been shaved to a buzz cut like Cody's.

"What happened to your hair?"

"I cut it with the horse clippers. What do you think?" Will's head was large and looked good with short hair. The crew cut was rough but made him look older and athletic.   "I like it."

"I got the idea when we trimmed the horse's manes. I couldn't get the back too good, so Sara helped finish it," Will said.

"Sara helped you?" he asked. So it wasn't Cody. That made

him feel better.

"I brought you a surprise."

He reached into the car and handed the lariat to Will. "I thought you'd enjoy owning a good rope."

"Cool!" Will made a loop and swung it over his head.

They heard a whinny and looked at a horse pacing back and forth in the corral.

"That's the stallion Harry bought. They delivered him this morning," Sara said. She disappeared inside the barn and then reappeared pushing a wheelbarrow loaded with two hay bales. She stacked one bale on top of another on the ground to approximate the height of a steer and then she stuck a plastic steer's head in the end of the top bale. Justin showed Will how to swing and throw the loop over the steer's horns. He stood with Sara, watching the boy try to rope the dummy steer.

"I'm glad you're back," Sara said.

"I'm happy to be home," he said.

She looked at him, smiled and started to say something when Will whooped — he'd roped the dummy.

"You do it, Dad."

Justin threw the rope and missed. He dropped the loop over the horns on his fifth try.

"You try, Sara," said Will.

She coiled the rope, formed a loop, swung it once over her head and dropped it over the steer's head.

"She's better than you, Dad."

"You'd better believe it."

As they watched Will throw the lariat, he put his arm around Sara's waist. She leaned into him and she felt good.

Will improved. Sara put the hay bale with the dummy in the wheel barrel and began pushing it at a walk. "See if you can rope a moving steer," she said.

Will threw the loop at the moving target until he was roping it half the time. Sara began pushing the wheel barrel faster. Will had to trot to be in position to rope it.

Justin took over and pushed the target even faster, so Will had to run and throw. Finally, laughing, they sat on the ground to catch their breath.

"Why don't you boys do a sleep-over tonight?" Sara asked.

He looked at Will. "It's up to you."

"Really?"

"Yeah, whatever you want," he said.

"That would be wicked!"

After dinner, they played Crazy Eights. Finally, Sara said, "Will, you can use my guest bedroom and your dad can sleep in Harry's room."

"It wouldn't be a real sleepover unless I slept with Will," Justin said, ignoring her fleeting glance.

"Is that okay with you, Will, or would you rather me sleep in Harry's room?"

"Whatever."

Justin laughed. "No, not whatever. You've got to make a decision — sleep with me or bunk alone."

"We've never bunked together. I'd like that."

Sara gave them robes and said goodnight. He and Will climbed into two double beds and turned off the light. He listened to his son's breathing and thought about how much he'd enjoyed playing with his son. Maybe he was learning how to be a father.

"Dad?"

"Yeah?"

"Do you ever get scared at night?"

"Yeah, sometimes a big bear chases me. Scares me to death," he said.

"Not to death."

"No, I wake up before it catches me, but I get really frightened," he said. "How about you. Do you get scared at night?"

"That's why I like to leave a light on."

"We'll fix that." He got up, turned the bathroom light on and left the door cracked. "Is that better?"

"Yeah." A few minutes later, Will said, "Dad? This is fun."

Later, he listened to Will's soft snoring for at least half an hour, making sure he was asleep. Then he slipped on a robe, tiptoed to the door and closed it behind him. There was a light on in the kitchen.

Sara, wearing a robe, turned and smiled at him. "Couldn't sleep."

"Me neither."

He pulled her to him and kissed her hard. She bit his lip. He tasted blood. She struggled and then relaxed and her lips responded. Their tongues touched. He hardened and she stroked him. His hand slipped under her robe and touched her breast. His fingers caressed a nipple that grew as hard as it had when they had made teenage love.

"No! Not here." She held his hand and led him to her bedroom. Passions rising, they shed their robes and stumbled into bed.

Bodies entwined, they kissed and he inhaled her scent, a blend of all that he had remembered and he knew he was again with the right woman. He kissed her nipples and then in between her breasts, enveloped by the musky smell he remembered. He slid his mouth down her belly, nibbling, kissing, down to caress her inner thighs and he raised his lips to brush her clitoris and inhaled the fruity scent from between her legs. He slowly retraced his movements until his lips were on hers and she was ready and he entered her, and then he smelled the dark primitive scent of her gasps. Later, he rolled onto his back and cradled her head in the crook of his elbow and stared at the beams and ceiling. After all these years, she was better than she had been. Better than his imagination. Better than any woman. Incredible. He wanted to stay with her forever.

After they had recovered, they went back into the kitchen.

She fixed cinnamon toast and poured glasses of milk. He lit a fire in the family room fireplace. She brought a tray with milk and toast and they sat on the couch.

"We're better than when we were young," he said.

"I feel like a dam has broken," she said. "Like I've waited for this a long time."

He agreed. "I had fun with you and Will this afternoon."

"It was wonderful. Did you have a productive trip?"

He stared into the flames and thought about how to put the best face on what he was going to say. He began talking, but evidently there wasn't a good face — she rose off the couch to face him.

"How could you sell out like that? How could you do that to your brother?"

"I've got Cody and Linda covered. It will be a fine development, a real asset to this area."

"Are you that dense?" she asked crossing her arms over her chest. "The new people will be people just like you."

"Like me?"

"I can't believe you'd develop your family ranch into a fortress for the rich. How could you?"

"What choice did I have?" he said.

"You're desecrating our entire valley for the sake of money? Why don't you just buy it?"

"If it means so much to you, why didn't you buy it from my dad?"

"I offered to help him with The Nature Conservancy and I suggested it to you as well. Both of you are so damned pigheaded you wouldn't listen."

He turned from her and put both hands on the mantle and stared into the flames until his anger subsided and then he turned to face her.

"You told me The Nature Conservancy didn't have the cash to buy it and even if they had the cash, it would take too long to cut a deal before the redemption deadline. If keeping this valley pristine is so important to you, why didn't you buy it as a bridge to the Nature Conservancy?"

"I can't take large principal sums from my trust. I live on the return from those investments," she said.

"So do I!"

"You're a Wall Streeter. You could have figured out something other than selling it to a damned developer, for God's sake!"

"I didn't have the time," he said.

"You could have borrowed short-term money from someone."

"I made the best decision I could. It wasn't my fault my old man got into financial trouble. I didn't know about the problem until the funeral. There wasn't time to do it any other way."

"Or you can't think about things any other way?"

"Let's not let this get between us. I'm sorry." He reached for her.

She shook him off. "You have no feelings for your family or this land. That's always been your problem."

"That's not fair!"

"Feelings are facts. I'm going to bed, and I want you gone in the morning, as in take-a-fly-on-your-jet gone."

Chapter 31

The next morning, they found Sara working on her laptop computer at the kitchen table. She closed the lid and smiled at Will. She looked at Justin and her smile faded. He fought an impulse to tell her that he was sorry for their argument.

Evidently, Will noticed as well. "Are you feeling okay, Sara?" he asked.

"I'm just a little tired, I didn't sleep well," she said.

"Why not?" Justin asked.

She shot him a look. "How did you boys sleep?"

"Great!" Will said.

"I had trouble sleeping," Justin said.

"Why?" Will asked.

"Because you snore as loud as an old bear." Justin reached over and rubbed Will's crew cut.

The boy grinned.

As they went out the door, Justin added, "I'm sorry about how last night ended."

"I am, too," she said. "What is it about you? I'm torn between desire and repulsion."

When they drove back to the ranch, Linda was on her hands and knees near the south wall of their cabin planting a garden. She rose to greet them.

"Here's a book Sara borrowed," Justin said.

"Oh my gosh, I have three of hers. I need to get them back." Linda tucked her gloves in her back pocket and then turned toward her cabin.

"Where's Cody?" Justin asked.

"He's down at Dark Lake. He wanted to see if the swan came back this spring," she said.

"I need to talk with him. Could Will hang with you for a while?" he asked.

"I'll make a gardener out of him."

Back at his cabin, in need of a clean shirt, Justin took one of his old man's red and white checked shirts from the closet and looked at it. He had destroyed the shed that contained the painful memories. His father was gone. The shed was gone. He'd learned about Miss Adams and his old man and that he was Miss Adams' son. That was all in the past. His old man couldn't scare him anymore. It was time to move on.

He put on his father's shirt. While buttoning it, he looked at the two pictures on the dresser. There was a crack in the glass of the picture of the woman he used to call his mother. He shook his head. He spotted the old man's Stetson on the closet shelf. He tried it on. It fit well enough. He'd wear it. He looked in the mirror and recoiled — he looked just like his old man.

Now dressed, he called Duncan in Manhattan. He told his future partner he'd be returning next week. They set a date to sign a partnership agreement.

He drove toward Dark Lake and thought about where to start with Cody. Was there any point to tell him about the photo album or the letter or that they were half-brothers? Cody claimed to have moved on from the loss of their mother. Claimed he never cared. It didn't make any sense that Justin, as a bastard child, would have been closer to their "mother" than the natural child. Cody. His "brother." So much taller. Such a different personality. Now it made sense.

But he needed to stay in the present. He had to convince

Cody to accept the ranch deal he'd cut with Gordon.

He patted his river stone when he spotted Cody sitting at the base of an ancient Douglas fir overlooking Dark Lake. The water mirrored five-hundred-foot limestone formations locals called Cathedral Cliffs. Thickets of black spruce surrounded the reed-edged lake.

When he approached, Cody nodded and then studied his face. "I'll be damned."

"What?"

"Never saw the resemblance before." Cody retrieved his tobacco can, opened the lid, took a pinch between his fingers and then stuck the chew between his lower lip and gum.

"What resemblance?"

"You're wearing our old man's hat — you look just like him."

He had his mother's eyes and now Cody said that he looked like their old man. Made sense — got his father's looks and Miss Adams' brains. He sat next to Cody and felt the warmth of his brother's shoulder. He leaned back against the massive tree trunk. Damp marsh scents mingled with the aroma of resin and needles and mint-flavored tobacco — his brother's habit.

Cody pointed to a white speck high above. "Here he comes."

A trumpeter swan, nine-foot-wings cupped, descended in a slow spiral toward the lake, white body reflecting from the water. The swan glided toward the surface, extended its feet and splashed down, creating ripples that distorted his reflection. An instant later, they heard the sound of the landing.

"He always returns about now. I try to greet him every spring," Cody said.

"How do you know it's a him?"

"He had a mate. They mate for life, you know."

"Everyone out here mates for life," Justin said. "What happened?"

"Don't know. Maybe she hit a power line. Hell, maybe she left him." Cody shot him a sideways glance.

"How long ago?" he asked.

"Six years. He comes back every year, spends the summer and then flies off at the first snow. I keep hoping he'll find another mate, but he never does. Just returns here, year after year. Alone."

They fell into silence and watched the swan.

"He sorta reminds me of you, Justin."

"How's that?"

"That swan, he's about the handsomest thing alive and yet he's all alone," Cody turned his head and spat a stream of juice.

"Maybe he likes being alone."

"Thought of that, but I watched them when he first brought his mate here. Watched them do their courting dance, watched them build their nest and watched them raise their young. Preened each other when they weren't teaching their kids. And then, after she was gone, I watched him come back all by himself. Nobody likes being alone. He must be sad. He's a lot like you."

"I'm not sad," Justin said.

"So you say."

He rubbed his neck. He didn't need his brother's damned judgments. As the swan swam closer, he tried to imagine flying thousands of miles back to its breeding area.

"Must have been a long, tiring trip."

"You should know, bro," Cody said.

"Where'd you pick up language like that?"

"We're uptown. Watch a lot of satellite TV in the winter. Even saw that Janet Jackson's titty at the Super Bowl Game. That woman must be packed with plastic."

He sorted through the multitude of things he needed to discuss with Cody and started with their mother/step mother.

"Did the old man leave anything about Mom?"

"Haven't really cleaned out his things. What sort of thing you looking for?" Cody asked.

"Something that would tell us what happened to her. Maybe he'd heard from her or maybe heard about where she'd gone."

"Nope," Cody said.

"Doesn't it bother you?"

"Figure I can't do nothing about it. She's been gone a long time. Now don't get me wrong, I missed her. Missed her something terrible at first, but after a while I got used to it. I don't think about her much anymore, except when I see that picture of her on dad's dresser," Cody said.

"Ever wonder why she left?"

"She was unhappy," Cody said.

"Ever wonder if something else might have happened to her?"

Cody spat and looked at him. "Like what?"

"You know."

"I never thought about that sort of thing. Won't do any good to dwell on it. What's done is done. Nothing we can do about it. Besides, it doesn't much matter anymore, does it? Our old man's gone and we got our own families. At least I do."

Listening to Cody made him feel raw and edgy. How could Cody have come to terms with losing his mother when he was so young? Why hadn't Justin moved on? Cody's willingness to accept their mother's disappearance was probably a cop-out. After all, they had grown up in a state of denial.

He watched the swan float alone on the black water. The bird swung its long neck in a white feather-clad loop and then tucked its head under its wing to sleep.

Cody broke into his thoughts. "Only thing I regret was how our old man treated you. Don't know why he took out his anger on you. I watched it, but there was nothing I could do. He drove you off the place and that wasn't right."

"Thanks," he said.

"After he quit drinking, he felt bad and wanted to apologize," Cody said.

"Why didn't he?"

"He made himself a promise that he'd apologize, but you'd have to call first. He was stubborn — a lot like you."

Justin flinched as though he'd been slapped.

"You left me, too," Cody said.

He glanced at Cody. The thought that his leaving the ranch would cause his brother to feel rejected had never crossed his mind. He'd always assumed . . . what the hell had he assumed? Cody had been the old man's favorite and never beaten. He seemed happy on the ranch. He'd never miss Justin. It had never occurred to him that he could have caused the same sort of hurt for his brother that their mom's leaving had created for him.

He rubbed his fingers through his hair and then massaged the back of his neck.

The swan, exhausted from its trip, slept.

A cloud blotted out the sun. A quick breeze ruffled the water's surface and then died. There was an eerie quiet.

Cody arced a stream of brown juice that splashed onto a pine cone.

"Figured out how we keep the ranch?"

He'd have to approach this in exactly the right way, take time to explain the situation so Cody would buy into the deal. Hell, any sane man would jump at the opportunity.

"Ever wonder why Kamm bought the certificate of redemption?"

"He already had the old man's personal loan. Had to protect his investment. Makes sense."

"He's planning to evict you from the ranch as soon as he takes over."

Cody jumped to his feet. "Like hell he will. I won't go!"

"Then you'll end up in jail."

"Don't give a damn!"

"Calm down and listen. I did some research on Kamm and

discovered he has a contract to sell the ranch to a developer. Kamm planned to flip the ranch and make millions."

"You're a goddamned liar. Kurt sell to a developer who'll cut our trees down and put up fancy houses and condos and stores and pave the whole goddamned place? Over my dead body!"

The swan's head slipped from under its wing, its long neck uncoiled and held its head high, alert for danger.

"Damnit, Cody, just listen before you fly off the handle."

"I'm not off flying off the handle. I'm just madder than hell. Kurt Kamm wouldn't do that."

"You're scaring the swan."

Cody looked at the swan. It paddled toward the far shore, head high, looking over his back toward them. "So what's your brilliant plan?"

"I've got a plan to help you stay on the place. Sit down and listen," Justin said.

"Don't tell me what to do!"

Justin stood up. "You do want to stay on the ranch, don't you?"

"You're damned right!"

"I met with the developer. It was a tough negotiation, but I cut a deal where you can stay on the place."

Cody's eyes clouded. "What do you mean, 'cut a deal'?"

"You want to stay on the ranch, but it has never provided a decent living. If I hadn't negotiated a deal with the developer, Kamm would buy the place and have the sheriff evict you. You wouldn't have a cent. You wouldn't have enough money to start over. You'd be screwed."

"Cut to the chase," Cody demanded.

"The bottom line is that you and Linda can stay on the ranch for the rest of your lives."

"What's the catch?"

"No catch. You'll have a lifetime job on the ranch at seventy-five-grand a year, plus you'll have seven million you can invest."

"What kind of work?"

"The kind of work you're good at. You'll build and maintain roads and look after the new houses and the owner's horses."

"You expect me to help a developer rape our ranch?" Cody screamed.

"It was the . . ."

"It'd be like destroying a church!"

The swan slipped into the reeds on the far shore and disappeared.

"Look, Cody, you can try it and if you decide you don't want to live on the ranch, you can take your millions and buy yourself a better place, land someplace that can produce a good living. Someplace with better winters that Linda would enjoy. You've got alternatives now. Before you had no choice."

"That's why you're so screwed up. It's all about money, isn't it? You can't see beyond the almighty buck!"

Justin clenched his fists. "You look at that damned swan out there and you have the nerve to compare that bird to me! You're the one who can't change, Cody. You're too fucking stupid to understand. You make a decision and are too proud to change your mind when the facts scream that you are making a mistake. Maybe you'll understand one of your own brainless sayings, 'Don't look a gift horse in the mouth'!"

"Fuck you!" Cody pushed him against the tree trunk with so much violence that it knocked his breath out.

Gasping for air, he sank to his knees and watched his brother stalk away.

Chapter 32

When he arrived, Sara stood next to the horse runs that extended from the barn. She watched the stallion push against the rails in an effort to get closer to the mare. She wore a Stetson, a doe skin vest over a white shirt, and tan chino chaps over her jeans.

She waved him over. "Is that your Dad's hat? You look just like him."

"So I've been told. Are you still angry with me about the ranch deal?" he asked.

"Yes, but I keep telling myself the world has to move on and that you've done the best you can. I don't know. It's so confusing."

He wrapped his arms around her and kissed her.

The stallion whinnied and reared and pawed the ground. The mare pranced back and forth along the wooden rails that separated them.

"He's acting like she's going into heat. I'd better get them separated," Sara said.

"Let's watch." He stepped behind her and slipped his arms around her.

"They'll throw a good foal." She took off her hat and leaned against him.

Her hair smelled of shampoo. He kissed her earlobe.

The stallion's hoofs struck a hollow sound on a lower fence rail. He snorted and then reared high. Slashing hooves splintered the top wood rail. The mare paced back and forth, watching the stallion struggle to get to her. The stallion reared again, thrashing his legs. His hooves crashed through the second rail. A splinter pierced his right leg. Blood flowed bright red.

Her body stiffened and pressed against him. "We're too late!"

The stallion leapt the lower rail and raced after the mare. Wild eyed, they neighed and frothed at the mouth. The stallion nipped the mare's neck.

He kissed her neck.

The stallion smelled the mare's heat.

He caressed her breasts.

The mare kicked at the stallion. He reared and then smelled her rear. A long pink tongue licked. She kicked again without intent.

She moaned.

The mare spread her legs, twisted her tail to the side. Her vulva pulsed wet and pink. The stallion's penis emerged from its sheath, black and hard.

She moved her hips against him.

The stallion pushed his chest against the mare's butt and then he reared, sliding his front hooves over her sides, his hips driving his shaft toward her opening.

She touched him.

The stallion's hind legs thrust his hips forward. The head of his shaft touched her lips.

He unzipped her pants and his fingers brushed her pubic hair and then caressed her clitoris.

The stallion's shaft plunged deep. His hips began a rhythmic motion. The mare threw her head and, the moment before climax, walked out from under the stallion. He stood in the middle of the run, hard and perplexed. He neighed, stretched his head forward and curled his lips over his teeth. He moved toward her. The mating dance began once again.

She turned and their lips met. A musky smell floated on her breath.

He led her into the barn, took her into his arms and kissed her. He slipped off her vest and then groped for her shirt buttons. He stripped off his shirt. He felt her naked breasts against his bare chest. She unzipped his pants. He unbuckled her chaps. She pushed him, stepped back, kicked off her boots and, leaving the chaps on, slipped out of her jeans and panties.

He ripped off his boots, socks and red paisley boxer shorts. Naked, but for his Stetson, he felt the barn's rough-cut planking under his feet. He kissed her, tongue probing. He recognized the scent that rose from her breath — the aroma he had been searching for since the last time they had made love.

She turned away and dropped to her hands and knees next to the stall. "Now!"

On his knees behind her, he cupped her breasts and felt her hand guide him into her.

The mare and stallion burst into the stall and sprayed wood shavings and the scent of fresh cut pine over them. The horses neighed and bit and spun. They slammed against the gate.

He began moving, slow deep thrusts that grew faster, she possessing him, he possessing her, his breath rasping, hers choppy moans.

The mare and stallion stared at them with wild eyes. Hooves slashed. The stallion mounted the mare. His shaft pounded deep and matched their rhythm. The horses neighed and whinnied.

His Stetson fell off. Splinters penetrated his knees. He groaned. Sara uttered a primal scream.

"Sara? Sara? Are you all right?" A voice called from outside the barn.

Sara scooted out from under him. "Oh, my God! It's Linda. Get dressed!"

The stallion slid off the mare and stood on wide front legs with his head down.

The voice was closer now. "Sara, are you hurt?"

Sara scooped up her clothes, fled into the tack room and shut the door. He scrambled for his clothes, his boxer shorts — where the hell were his boxers? No time. Hell with them.

The stallion mounted the mare again.

Linda's footsteps crunched closer on the gravel driveway. He tucked in his shirt, jammed on boots, and threw his socks in an empty water bucket and then slipped into his boots.

"Sara?" Linda shouted over the noise of the mating horses.

He jammed on the Stetson as Linda walked around the corner of the barn door. The hat felt odd . . . on backward.

"Hello, Linda."

She stopped and pressed several books to her chest.

He nodded toward the stallion and mare, "We were watching."

"Uh-huh." Linda's face broke into a grin and then she pointed to something at his feet. "Better hide them quick-like."

His boxer shorts hung from inside his right pant, covering the toe of his boot.

"Oh, shit!" He stripped the boxers from his pant leg and held them in his hand.

"In your hat!" Linda whispered.

He ripped off his hat, stuffed the boxers in the crown and set the Stetson back on his head, correctly this time. It sat high. He squished it down.

Sara walked out of the tack room looking as if nothing had happened. "I thought I heard your voice, Linda."

"Phones are down. I drove down to say you two are welcome to join us for dinner. Since I was coming, I thought I'd return these." Linda gave the books to Sara.

"Aren't you sweet," Sara said.

"Thought I heard you screaming for help," Linda said.

Sara laughed. "We were cheering the stallion and mare on. Guess we got carried away."

Linda grinned. "I'm thinking it's not a good time for a dinner invite. Should I tell Will that his dad's going to stay the night?"

Justin glanced at Sara. She nodded.

He walked Linda back to her truck and opened the door for her.

She winked and whispered, "Ride'em, cowboy!"

He watched Linda drive off. Sara squeezed his waist and said, "I've fantasized about that."

"Me too," he said, not knowing if her fantasy was making love wearing chaps, doing it doggie-style, doing it in the barn, getting caught, or doing it next to mating wild horses. Hell, he was so happy it didn't matter what she meant. He put his arm around her and they walked toward her house to clean up.

After his shower, he brushed off his clothes and put them back on. He wished for a clean shirt. The jeans scraped against splinters buried in his knees. Several minutes later, he walked into the family room and he looked at a new Sara, dressed in a red sheath and high heels. Her lips were painted. He couldn't remember her wearing lipstick. Mascara shadowed her eyes and emphasized her eyelashes. She'd pulled her hair into a French twist, which exposed the nape of her neck.

She walked toward him. Even her stride was different – like that of a fashion model strutting a catwalk. She'd knock them dead in Manhattan. She stood close. He smelled a new scent, perfume.

"Like to dance?" she asked.

"Love it," he lied. Thank God Ashley had insisted he take dance lessons.

She put on a CD and waited for him.

His fantasies about her had never included dancing, but he wanted this to be perfect. He put his arm around her and took her hand. He felt awkward for a moment before the pulse of the music seized his mind and guided his feet and he felt light and graceful and in love.

Chapter 33

At dawn the next morning, he woke with her head nestled in the crook of his arm. He snuggled closer. A gurgle rose from her throat.

"That's nice," he whispered.

"Um-mmm."

He drifted to sleep feeling whole and complete. The person he loved was in his arms.

Sometime later, he stirred to her fragrance. For the first time when he'd been with a woman, he didn't want to jump out of bed, get dressed and move on. He'd be happy to lie there with her forever. His fingers caressed her hip and stomach, and he felt a patch of striations on her skin. He ran his fingertips over them and realized they were stretch marks. He wished he'd seen her big with Harry. He wished he'd been there for her.

A few minutes later, she turned to him. "What was Cody's reaction to your agreement with the developer?"

He wished she hadn't brought up that subject. "He'll be all right once he thinks it through. It's a great deal for him."

"Uh-huh." She turned her head away from him and looked out the window.

"Are you still upset about it?"

"I keep trying to tell myself that it's all right, that we are just caretakers of the earth and the world has to move on, but I still can't help but feel that it is the wrong thing to do for this valley. I'm very sad about it."

All he could think of saying was that he was sorry and he wished he could have found a better solution, but there were no words that would make her feel better.

He got dressed. He had pulled several splinters, but obviously there were more, because his knees burned against the rough fabric of his jeans. He told Sara he had to get back to Will before he left for the weekend with Cody and Linda in Missoula. She agreed to take an afternoon ride with him to their favorite spot on the Squaw Creek Trail where they'd first made love.

Driving into the ranch, he spotted Will walking up the driveway to irrigate the upper pasture. The boy wore calf-high rubber boots and carried a shovel over his shoulder.

Justin stopped. "I'll help you irrigate."

They walked into the upper pasture. A few early wildflowers dotted the short grass, splotches of purple and yellow and white.

They found the first tarp, an orange plastic sheet attached to a five-foot pole. The tarp's corners had been shoveled deep into each bank of the ditch to form a dam. Water pooled and spilled over the bank to flood about thirty yards of pasture.

"I'll get it, Dad." Will pulled up one corner of the plastic and watched as water burst under the dam and gushed with a splashing roar down the ditch. They laughed.

They dragged the tarp sixty yards down the ditch. Will swung the pole across and pulled the tarp over the surface of the moving water and then he stepped on the plastic to force it against the bottom. Justin rolled several large rocks on the leading edge so water couldn't work its way under the plastic and then Will shoveled the edges of the tarp into the ditch to prevent leakage and eventual blowout.

They leaned on their shovels shoulder to shoulder and watched water back up, rise to the top of the bank and then spill over to irrigate thirsty earth.

"We done good," Will said.

"You're beginning to talk like your uncle."

"Think so?" Will asked.

"Yes, he's a good guy." But he could be one stubborn son-of-a-bitch, he added under his breath.

After they set the tarps in the upper pasture, they found a dry spot in the sun and lay on their backs in sweet grass and listened to the buzz of insects pollinating wildflowers.

Justin looked at his son. "You're growing up."

"I like it here better than New York."

"Why?"

"People teach me things. There's a lot to do."

"What about Mom?"

"She'd hate it here."

"Is that a problem?"

He shrugged.

A red-tail hawk carved slow circles overhead. Ravens, perched in a tree at the edge of the pasture, cawed back and forth.

"You're busy when you're in New York," Will said.

"I'm sorry about the divorce, Will. It wasn't your fault."

"Most of the kids at school have parents who are divorced and they don't care. At least they pretend they don't. I like it here. Can I stay?"

"I'll think about it." He didn't want to ruin the moment by saying they'd be returning next week. There was no way he'd leave Will out here.

They lay next to each other, silent. Another red-tail hawk joined the one overhead and they floated in lazy circles. They were mates.

Finally, Will stood up and said, "Let's ride after we finish irrigating."

At the barn, Justin and Will saddled Baily and Jake. They played horse-tag in the corral until the horses were lathered with sweat. They reined up to give the horses a rest.

"Did you play tag with your dad?"

"My old man was too busy to play. We roped calves during branding."

"That'd be fun," Will said.

He looked at his watch. "Linda will have lunch ready soon. We'd better put up the horses."

After they unsaddled, Jake raised his head high to let Justin brush crusted-over insect bites on his chest.

"Jake really likes you," Will said.

"I like him, too. He's got good sense and I trust him."

"He trusts you, too," Will said.

Back at the cabin, Justin helped Will pack for the weekend in Missoula. Justin found Linda in the kitchen packing for their trip. He sat down stiff-legged so his jeans wouldn't rub against the splinters in his knees.

She walked into the bathroom. When she returned, she gave him a pair of tweezers and a magnifying glass.

"What's that for?" he asked.

"Thought you might want to pull some splinters."

"What?"

"Been there and done that!" she said with a mischievous grin.

Cody and Will walked into the kitchen, sat down and began to eat sandwiches Linda had prepared.

"Eat up. We've gotta leave for Missoula," Cody said.

"Sure you won't change your mind, Justin?" Linda said.

"No, I want to stick around in case Sara needs help with her new stallion."

Linda grinned.

After lunch, they packed the truck and stood by the driver's door while Justin said goodbye to Will, who then jumped into the back seat and slammed the door. Otto paced in the bed of the truck, growling and keeping an eye on Justin.

Cody turned to him. "Your mind still set the way it was when we were down at Dark Lake?"

"It's for the best," Justin said.

"Figures."

"What in the world are you two talking about?" Linda asked.

"Didn't he tell you about the ranch?" Justin asked.

Linda looked at Cody.

"As soon as Justin redeems the ranch Monday, he's gonna sell it to a developer quicker than beer turns into piss. My son-of-a-bitch brother sold us down the river."

"Why didn't you tell me before?" Linda asked Cody.

"Hoped he'd change his mind, and spare you the hurt, but I should of known better." Cody climbed behind the driver's seat.

Linda gave Justin a disgusted look, got in the truck and then slammed the door.

Will looked at him out the back window, as he watched them drive down the driveway and disappear.

Chapter 34

Justin and Sara trailered their horses under a bright blue sky to the Squaw Creek Trailhead. He mounted Jake and took the lead as they rode up through switchbacks into the wilderness area.

Far below, the creek reflected through holes in the green canopy of a spruce forest. The sun was alive over the mountains — the light waved and shone, and mirrored distant objects. Up in this high air he breathed easily and, for the first time, he became conscious that it was the vital quality of the air in these mountains that made him feel alive.

The trail topped out into a small fragrant meadow and then rose again, climbing above the cliffs that rimmed the valley.

An hour later, Justin reined up under a Douglas fir. Twenty miles west, at the headwaters of Squaw Creek, snow-capped peaks shimmered in the light. He hobbled the horses to let them graze and then found Sara leaning against the massive tree, arms crossed and boot jacked back against the trunk.

He picked a magenta shooting star and handed it to her.

She smiled at the flower and brushed it against her cheek.

"I picked a shooting star for you on our first picnic here."

"I remember."

He leaned against the tree next to her and their shoulders brushed. This was the right place to bring her. His fingers brushed his river stone. "Remember everything?"

"We were young and eager, and that was a lifetime ago."

"You were my first. I've thought about you ever since."

She smiled and her fingertips brushed the back of his hand.

"Remember our first time? Here? Under this tree?" He needed her to say yes to the easy questions, so it would be easier for her to say yes to the important questions.

She leaned her head against the tree trunk and watched an eagle flare high in the thin mountain air to meet another eagle. The birds closed on each other at a fierce speed. One eagle tucked its left wing under its body and rolled and they locked talons. They fell, wings tucked together, falling faster and faster until they disappeared over the edge of the cliff.

"Do you think they'll survive?" she asked.

"That's the way I feel every time I'm with you," he said.

"That's sweet."

"What do you feel?" he asked.

"We were young, clumsy but enthusiastic. We're more experienced now."

"Still enthusiastic?" he asked.

A small laugh gurgled in her throat. "More appreciative."

He sought her lips. She pushed him away. "Not now."

"Why not?"

"We can't recreate our youth. We're in different places now."

"I wonder what those lost years could have been. Had I known you were pregnant, our lives would have been so different."

She laughed. "You're pretty sure of yourself. I might not have married you."

"I might not have asked." He said with a smile meant to assure her he was kidding. "Seriously, I made a mistake when I let you go the first time. Why don't you come back to Manhattan with me?

She looked startled.

He rushed on, "We could do the museums and go to the theater and great restaurants. We could go dancing. You love to dance. I love dancing with you."

"Just exactly what are you asking?"

"We missed our chance the first time. Let's not miss it again. Let's get married."

"I don't think that would be a good idea."

"Don't decide now. Just think about it. We can talk about it again tomorrow."

"I have appointments in town. I won't be back until evening."

"I'll keep you company," he said.

"No. I need to think about it."

"Promise to call me as soon as you get back."

"We'd better head back before it gets dark."

They mounted and he followed her back down the trail. They returned to her ranch, unsaddled and brushed the horses and turned them out to pasture. She closed the gate and then spun to face him. Her fingers dug into his arms.

"What gives you the right to walk into my life and toss it upside down? I was happy before you came here. I knew what I wanted. You have the nerve to get in the middle of everything and screw it up."

"Don't make a decision we'll both regret. Give us more time."

"Damn you, Justin! Go home. I'll call you tomorrow evening."

Chapter 35

Alone at the ranch the next morning, he picked shards of glass from the picture of his mother and then put it next to the photograph of Miss Adams. All the women he'd loved had betrayed him, or in Sara's case, he had been the betrayer. Not a good track record. He had to do something active or he'd go crazy waiting for Sara's call that evening.

He jammed on his old man's Stetson, tied a silk scarf around his neck and walked outside. He walked along the riverbank and watched the currents swirl, bringing back a forgotten memory. When he'd been a child, he rode with his mother into the high country, and they sat and talked at a wonderful place she called her favorite. He wondered if he could find it after all these years.

At the barn, he gathered a halter and walked to the corral where the horses stood sleeping in the morning sun. Jake's ears perked up and he walked to greet Justin. He scratched the buckskin's head.

"Well, Jake, looks like it's just you and me today." The horse's velvet smooth nose nuzzled his cheek.

After saddling Jake, he rolled a slicker and tied it behind the saddle. He found the pistol and gun belt above the rafter. The cartridge belt loops were empty. There were only three bullets in the revolver's cylinder. He searched the barn, but could find no more cartridges. Three would have to be enough. He strapped the gun belt on and then he took a lighter from the workbench. In the small refrigerator where Cody kept veterinary drugs, he found two Snickers bars, which he tossed into the saddlebag.

He loaded Jake into a trailer hitched to Linda's truck. He drove out of the ranch, turned left and drove high above tree line to the end of the road. The area looked vaguely familiar. He led Jake out of the trailer, tightened the saddle's cinch, mounted up and nudged the horse forward. Jake didn't whinny, which made him happy — most horses were herd bound and were nervous when alone. Jake was calm and responsive like all the ranch's horses. He had to give Cody credit for being a great horse trainer.

He felt the heat of the sun on his back as he urged the horse on to nowhere. Spring beauties poked through the grass. Patches of snow piled in the shadows of boulders. He followed a game trail that wove through meadows and krummholtz, deformed by the wind. Grizzlies used those stunted clumps of trees for day beds. He reined Jake into the open to avoid a nasty surprise. He rode over a crest of a hill and spotted bear tracks. Claw marks extended several inches in front of the toe pads. They were the largest set of grizzly tracks he had seen. It was an immense male, a boar. Like his nightmare bear.

He'd been inadvertently following the beast. He scanned the country ahead and spotted nothing. Clear water pooled in the tracks; the water would have been muddy had the bear been close. More than likely the bear was long gone; grizzlies could cover as many as thirty miles a day.

He rode through country that seemed familiar, yet he couldn't remember when he'd been there. Hours later he stopped on a south-facing ridge that looked over miles of mountains and the valley where the ranch lay and he realized he'd been there before. Thirty yards below, a massive Douglas fir grew on a wide grassy ledge perched on top of sheer cliffs. Now he remembered. He'd ridden here with his mom when he'd been a small boy.

She'd told him it was her favorite place.

He dismounted on the ridge top and tied Jake's halter rope to a dead branch of a wind-dwarfed pine. Remembering the bear tracks, he checked the revolver's cylinder again. He felt the loops of the cartridge belt. Empty. He should have gone back to the cabin, found a box of bullets and loaded the cartridge belt and revolver. Too late now. He took the Snickers bars from the saddlebag and then skidded down the slope and sat under the tree.

He leaned against the trunk and savored the taste of chocolate and watched two red-tailed hawks circle over the forest below. Everything was mating. He wondered if Sara would agree to marry him. He hoped so. He looked for familiar landmarks on the horizon – Coulter Mountain and Squaw Peak.

He sensed a difference in the air. The sky, that had been a vivid blue, was now soft and pallid. On the far western horizon, clouds gathered, towered high, sailing on strong winds.

They formed into a fast-moving mass with dark-rolling bottoms. A cold breeze hit his neck. Lost in thought about Sara, he didn't read the change in the weather. Instead, his fingertips, mindlessly working the earth, had traced irregular edges of a circle through which grass grew. They traced the circle again, and then another circle — a second circle?

He pushed the grass away and looked at a smooth white object. It was not a rock, definitely not rock. Bone. Grass grew through eye sockets.

He dug out a skull and brushed it off and studied it. Perhaps it was a skull of an Indian or cowboy or an early trapper.

His mother had brought him here to her favorite place when he was young. They had sat under this same tree and she had talked, but he couldn't remember her words.

He put the skull down and dug in the grass below where it had been hidden. His fingers touched something hard. He brushed debris from metal. He lifted a silver locket. He opened it and looked at his grandmother's picture. Or maybe she really wasn't his grandmother. Maybe she was Cody's grandmother, not his. He'd never know.

He closed the locket and pressed it to his chest. He rolled to his knees and moaned.

His first memory was of his mother holding him. Or had those been Miss Adams' arms? No, it was his mother's embrace he remembered. Wasn't it? He felt her warmth and her soft voice. Later, she sat on his bed and sang him to sleep. That wasn't Miss Adams. He remembered her swollen belly and later he watched her holding his screaming red wrinkle-faced baby brother whom he was forced to love even when he wanted to hit it. He shivered and pulled his collar close to his neck.

He remembered her fixing Thanksgiving dinners. Sewing torn jeans. Kissing hurt spots away. Her defeated eyes watching as his old man took him to the shed. Then that last night before she disappeared, she walked into their bedroom, sat on his bed and kissed him. She told him to remember that she loved him. He had watched through partially closed eyes, while she crossed to Cody's bed and kissed his brother's cheek. He wondered if Cody was also pretending to sleep. And then she was gone.

In the midst of trying to remember everything, he failed to notice heavy snow falling outside the circle of the tree's branches. He placed the skull back into the grass. He thought about taking the silver locket, but he didn't want to fight Cody over who would keep it. He placed the locket below her skull where it belonged and covered them with debris.

When she was covered, he said goodbye.

As if in a trance, he walked from under the shelter of the tree into calf deep snow. He snapped out of it when he looked up at a blizzard roaring past the lip of the ridge.

He had been foolish to get into this situation, stupid to ignore the warning signs. He knew about violent spring blizzards from his youth, he'd been trapped many times, forced to stay in town with Miss Adams, or snowbound at the ranch. Maybe this is what happened to his mother. She could have been trapped at her favorite spot and froze to death under the Douglas fir.

He began to climb the slope toward Jake. He slipped and fell and, by the time he stopped sliding through wet snow, he was soaked. He crawled back up to the ridge into the face of the spring blizzard and found the dwarfed tree where he'd tied the horse.

Jake was gone.

Chapter 36

Justin tugged his hat low to protect his eyes from stinging snow and examined the tree where he'd tied the horse. The limb was broken, the snow underneath trampled. The grizzly could have attacked Jake. He kicked the snow aside. There was no blood. The tracks were far apart. Jake had galloped away unharmed. Most likely, the horse had spooked from the bear's scent.

He had to follow the horse, catch him, and ride back to the truck, wherever it might be. The horse could find it, even in a blizzard — he hoped. The tracks led into the face of the blizzard. He needed to get back to redeem the ranch on Monday. What was today — Saturday? He had one day to get the hell off this mountain or they'd lose the ranch.

He hunched his shoulders against the cold and leaned against the wind into the whiteout. Soon a cloak of ice crystals covered him. Snow blew over the horse's tracks until they grew faint. If he didn't find Jake soon, he'd succumb to hypothermia and freeze to death. Rivulets of snow melt coursed under his collar and ran down his back. He tucked numb fingers under his arms and stumbled after the tracks until he spotted a semi-circle tunnel through the snow that looked like it had been made by the body of a bear.

He pulled the revolver from the holster, opened the cylinder to make certain a cartridge would be in the firing chamber when he pulled the trigger. He remembered his old man's words, "Save the last for yourself."

He pushed harder. His body warmed from plowing through the snow. He lost the tracks. He shielded his eyes from whirling snow and for an instant thought he saw a shadow.

Jake . . . or the bear?

He stumbled forward, revolver in both hands, praying it was not a mirage, praying it was Jake.

The image took form gradually. Jake faced him, head down, tail against the storm. Justin slipped the revolver into its holster and stumbled forward. Jake nickered. He grabbed the frozen halter rope, untied the slicker from behind the saddle and tried to put it on. The wind billowed the slicker. It snapped, making a loud popping noise. Jake leapt forward and pulled him on his back through the snow, his body corkscrewing. If he let go of the halter, he might never catch Jake again. Snow filled his eyes and ears and mouth.

The horse stopped and Justin brushed off and put on the slicker that mashed the cold wet clothes against his shivering body. He felt the warmth of the horse's body and smelled its wet hair when he tightened the cinch. He mounted up, slipped the halter rope under the pommel, hooked it around the horn and then picked up frozen reins.

"Okay, Jake, let's get out of this mess. Find the truck." He turned Jake in the direction of the truck, he hoped — he had no idea where it was. He nudged the horse forward into the face of the storm.

Jake took a few steps and then spun away from the stinging snow. Horses always wanted to turn away from blowing rain or snow. Justin tried again and again, but the horse refused to turn into the blizzard.

Maybe the horse would travel downwind toward the shelter of thick timber where he could build a fire before he froze to death. He kicked Jake in the ribs. The horse responded and plowed through deepening snow. He tucked the fingers of his hands between the saddle blanket and Jake's steaming shoulder.

Freezing in the saddle, he saw images of his mother's skull, the silver locket and his father's ghost. Once, when the wind shifted, he smelled cordite from the revolver — a bitter smell for bitter memories.

Jake walked for hours before he stopped, dropped his head close to the ground, his breath creating whirlwinds of snow. Justin slapped him with the reins. The horse dropped to his knees and then struggled up, but refused to move. The wind howled, driving sheets of snow against Justin's back. Mind numb, he huddled in the saddle, cold and wet. He began shivering again, his mind drifted into a hypothermic fantasy — he lay naked and warm on a sand beach. Blue waves beckoned. He drifted toward sleep.

He snapped back to reality — if he didn't warm up quickly he'd sink into the oblivion of death. He remembered reading a story about two hunters caught in a blizzard. In order to stay alive, they shot their horses, gutted them and then crawled inside the carcasses so they would not freeze to death. He shuddered. He dismounted and pulled on the reins to lead Jake forward. The horse refused. He slapped Jake on the butt and screamed. The exhausted animal would not budge.

"You have to get us out of here, Jake. If we don't get to shelter soon, we're going to freeze to death. I can't find the way, but you can."

He mounted the horse and nudged it with his heels. When Jake refused to move, he kicked him in the ribs. Jake trod forward several yards and stopped. He tried every trick he knew to get the horse to move. He got off and pulled the reins. Jake fell to his knees and then struggled up. Jake was exhausted and could go no further. He petted the horse's nose. He wished he had a dog sled team — he could have turned the sled over for shelter and then snuggled underneath with the dogs to keep warm and survive. There was no way to snuggle with a horse.

He unsaddled Jake, threw the blankets on top of the saddle and then traced an imaginary line from Jake's right ear to left eye, another line from the left ear to right eye and then he put the index finger of his left hand on the X where the two lines intersected on Jake's forehead. He aimed the muzzle of the revolver at the spot and then withdrew his finger.

He cocked the pistol. The horse looked at him through ice-rimmed eyelashes, trusting eyes brown and deep and calm.

"I'm sorry."

He held the gun at arm's length and squeezed the trigger. The explosion deafened him and the muzzle flash momentarily blinded him. Jake crashed on his side in the snow. Justin knelt and put his hand on Jake's neck and felt muscles quiver in relaxation of death.

"Two bullets left," he mumbled as he slid the revolver back into its holster. When Jake's spasms stopped, he pulled out his Leatherman Tool, opened the knife blade and locked it into place. Feeling for the place where Jake's last two ribs joined near the belly, he sliced a shallow hole through the skin, inserted two fingers of his left hand as a guide to keep the point of the blade from puncturing the guts and cut a straight line to the pelvis.

The blade punctured the lining and sour gas gushed out. He gagged. He reached inside the cut, around the stomach and liver and pulled part of the intestines outside the cavity and then forced his arm deep toward the neck to cut the innards away from the chest cavity. His hands were wet and warm. He cut the esophagus, which he squeezed shut to keep foul green contents from spilling, and then he used both hands to pull the gut pile into the snow.

It was nearly dark. There was little blood inside the steaming cavity. He picked up the saddle blankets, shook snow from them and piled them on top of the carcass, near the slit in its stomach. His first thought was to crawl inside head first, but his feet would have less chance of freezing in the thick chest area, and he'd be better able to breathe if his face was close to the opening, so he crawled feet first inside Jake's carcass. The slicker bound around his waist. His upper body was still freezing wet. The heat from the carcass would not dry him unless he stripped off the slicker. He pulled the saddle blankets inside the cavity, and then used the slicker to cover the opening.

Inside the carcass, the pungent odor of guts and blood made him gag. After some deep breathes, the stink disappeared — or he got used to it. He attempted to find the best position to wait out the blizzard and, after a series of contortions, he spread one blanket under him and used the other to cover his upper body. He maneuvered the slicker on top to keep out the snow.

In a fetal position inside the horse, hand grasping his river stone, he absorbed the warmth of the carcass. Outside the wind howled and snow assaulted the slicker. He'd have to keep checking to make certain he wasn't buried alive.

He repeated a mantra, "I'm going to make it. I'm going to make it."

Images of Sara flickered through his mind — her smile, the touch of her hand, the warmth of her body. Other images morphed with those visions — white skulls and silver lockets. His mother's smile morphed onto Sara's lips. Miss Adams' eyes stared at him through the white eye sockets of his mother's skull. Crazed with grief, wet and cold, he fell into exhausted sleep.

Sometime later, the wind stopped. He crawled out. Snow floated straight down. He held the slicker over his head while he tromped the snow around the carcass so it wouldn't cover him. He was much colder. He couldn't tell if the temperature had dropped or he was colder because of inactivity. He looked at his watch: 3:35 a.m. He crawled back inside and tried to sleep. He knew that within hours the carcass would freeze solid and he might be trapped inside. He'd start moving at daylight. He drifted to sleep.

Several hours later, in the leaden gray of dawn, his eyes snapped open with fear.

Chapter 37

The carcass shook. Justin heard snarling and the ripping of flesh. The sounds sparked images of his nightmare bear. He slipped the revolver from the holster and then raised a corner of the slicker and smelled fetid breath. He stared into a black face smeared with blood. White fangs. A torn ear in the shape of a capital M. Golden-yellow eyes stared at him — a wolf. The lone wolf he'd seen on Dead Man's Pass. It bared its teeth.

Justin shook the slicker at its face. The wolf skittered through the snow and then turned and snarled at him.

Could he kill the wolf with one bullet?

The wolf cocked its head, puzzled by the head that peered from the belly of the horse. It growled and took a step toward him. He aimed the pistol and then lowered it. Justin grasped the yellow slicker and waited. The wolf stalked closer.

"Yea-a-a-a-a-h!" He sprang up and snapped the slicker, making sharp sounds like shots.

The wolf spun, ran and then turned, fangs bared. Justin charged, flapping the slicker overhead. Looking over its shoulder, the wolf scrambled away.

Justin stumbled and fell into the snow and struggled to rise. The wolf turned and charged. Justin rose and snapped the slicker at the wolf's face. The wolf spun on immense paws and fled.

Screaming, Justin sprinted after the animal. Finally, it fled to a knoll fifty yards away where it sat and watched him, waiting for a sign of weakness.

Justin had read that wolves wouldn't kill humans. He'd believed that then. Not now. Now he understood wolves were predators, killing machines. They might be afraid of a healthy man, but if a wolf was hungry and found a sick or dying human, he'd do what he was born to do — kill and eat. It was the law of survival. Wolves were no different than humans and that's why men feared them.

Justin scooped a handful of snow into his mouth. It melted into a trickle of ice water. He couldn't eat too much snow, because it would cool his body and he couldn't get any colder and function. On the other hand, if he didn't get enough liquid, he would dehydrate, go into shock and die. He didn't have much time.

Justin stood next to the carcass and looked at the sky. It had cleared directly above, but the blizzard hovered to the south. Search planes couldn't fly. The storm had probably knocked out the phone lines, so Sara couldn't call for help. Will was with Cody and Linda in Missoula. He was on his own.

The rising sun painted Coulter Mountain a delicate pink.

The wolf wouldn't wait forever. Justin couldn't stay with the carcass. He had to get back today. He had to walk out, but could he make it?

He needed food and water, and something to keep him from freezing to death. He pulled a saddle blanket from inside the carcass. It was bloody, but wool retained body warmth even when wet. He sliced a hole in its center and slipped it over his head like a Mexican serape. He needed to tie it close to his body so heat wouldn't escape through open sides. He post-holed through snow toward the buried saddle and realized he couldn't make it back to the ranch without snowshoes.

He found the saddle, still pliable under the insulating snow. He cut leather tie strings off the saddle to make a belt and then tied the serape close to his body. He cut the saddlebags apart and then pulled one over each boot and lashed them to his heels and legs to make snowshoes. Other leather strings bound the cuffs of his pants to keep out snow.

He returned to the carcass and found the entrails. He used the Leatherman's blade to cut off the stomach and a short length of intestine. He turned the stomach inside out, cleaned it with snow and then turned it again and packed it with clean snow. He tied it into a loop with a rawhide string and then slipped it over his shoulder and under the cloak. After his body heat melted the snow, he'd have water to drink.

He glanced at the wolf, watching from the knoll. He cut off the two tenderloins from the inside of Jake's rib cage. He now had more meat than he needed if everything went well, but he'd need extra food if he broke a leg and waited days before he was found . . . if he was found alive.

He sliced a hole through the ends of the tenderloins and tied them with a saddle string and then slung that loop of meat over his other shoulder.

He put on his Stetson and squinted through blinding sunshine that now reflected off snow. His eyes watered. He would go snow blind without sunglasses. He unknotted the black scarf and sliced eye slits. He tied it around his head.

He surveyed the carnage before waving to the wolf. "It's all yours. Eat well and leave me the hell alone."

As Justin snowshoed toward Coulter Mountain, the wolf slunk toward Jake's carcass.

The wind blew against his face as he staggered though deep snow. Later, he heard a rasping sound. Two ravens, black feathers shining in the sunshine, circled overhead and cawed to each other as if they were discussing him. Some Native Americans held the raven sacred, believing they contained great wisdom and magical powers, but he thought they were just big crows.

Hours later, he found a windblown rocky knob. The branches of a dwarf tree provided tinder for a fire and he warmed his hands near the flames. Memories flitted across his mind but he had no energy to spare to dwell on them. He felt a sensation of being watched. He stood and looked, but saw nothing but snow.

He cut off a chunk of tenderloin, speared it on a green branch and held it over the fire. When the meat sizzled brown, he gripped one end with his teeth and used the knife to cut off a bite-sized piece and began to chew. He realized he was eating Jake and he gagged and spit the meat into the fire. He had no choice. He had to kill Jake or he would have died. The horse would have died sooner or later. Jake's death now served a better purpose than living until it was old and crippled and then being slaughtered by a canner, the fate of most horses. He needed energy. Eating was a matter of survival. He had to get back. He cut another piece of meat. It was hot and tender and good and he licked hot juices from his fingers.

He drank water, refilled the canteen with snow, warmed his hands and then curled into a ball next to the fire and slept. Sometime later, cawing awakened him. The ravens circled overhead, gliding on wind currents.

He rose, shouldered the remaining meat, and trudged through the snow toward Coulter Mountain. Sun reflected off the snow, making it warmer.

The ravens circled overhead. Their raucous cawing sounded like laughter — but that was impossible. He was going crazy, he thought, as he plowed through the snow toward home.

That evening, he stood on top of sheer limestone cliffs, exhausted but hopeful — he recognized familiar landmarks above the vision quest spot.

The afternoon sun had melted the snow along the edge of the cliffs, so he pulled the scarf from his eyes and wrapped it around his neck for warmth and then he cut off the makeshift snowshoes.

The ranch beckoned far away, below the cliffs. He imagined

the warmth of the wood stove, smells of baking bread and frying bacon, and the sound of Sara's laughter. Even though the
sun shone low over Coulter Mountain, the blizzard continued to
smother Dead Man's Pass.

He spotted the ravine that led down to the Indian vision
quest site. He would not have time to climb down the cliffs below the vision quest spot before dark and it would be too dan-
gerous to attempt it after dark. He would fall to his death. He
would have to spend the night there. He lurched toward a lone
Douglas fir that marked the way down.

The ravens cupped their wings and perched on a high branch
of the tree. He glanced up at the birds, stumbled, and fell. He lay
in soft duff and fought a temptation to sleep and wondered if
he was already asleep — was this a nightmare? He struggled to
his feet and lurched toward the tree. Shafts of twilight filtered
through tree branches.

A few minutes later, he scrambled down the ravine to the
vision quest place. Winds corkscrewed around the edge of the
cliffs, but it was calm on the wide ledge. He looked at the fifty-
foot diameter ring of rocks and the line of smaller rocks that
formed an arrow that cut through the center of the circle. He
remembered the morning he had been there with Sara as the
summer solstice sun exploded from the mountaintop.

The horizon was a thin silver line silhouetting Coulter
Mountain. As darkness fell, the peak flattened and smoothed, as
if the mountain was stretching out for a long night's sleep.

He snapped off dead twigs and branches from a nearby pine
and placed them in a fire pit built between the quest circle and
the granite wall that rose to the top of the cliff.

He remembered reading Jack London's story to Will, so he
made certain that the fire pit was not under a snow-laden pine
branch.

He held the lighter under the kindling and snapped its flint
several times before the flame fluttered to life. The twigs and

small branches ignited and he piled on larger pieces. Soon fire-light lit the Indian place under a canopy of stars.

He stood close to the fire and the warmth of the flames dissolved his tension into the night air. He sat on the ground, leaned against the rock wall and rested.

He skewered a piece of tenderloin on a green stick and held it over the fire to cook. He thought about Will and Sara and selling the ranch so Cody could stay on it for the rest of his life. He'd tried, but no one was happy. Why couldn't he make anyone happy? Even Will. He thought about how he'd struggled the last few days to have a relationship with his son, yet the boy seemed to like Cody and Linda better. Will didn't want to return to Manhattan. Sara wasn't enthused about marriage and reluctant to go back with him. He had to go back. His life was there.

He ate and then piled dead branches on the dying coals. Flames leapt high. Shadows danced across the site. He warmed his hands and felt welcome heat on his face and legs. The horse blanket serape steamed and reeked of blood and gore and death.

After he'd grown accustomed to the stench, he leaned back against the sloping rock and looked up through a vast darkness to the shining and glittering of thousands of stars, the Milky Way, winding through the night in an endless stream. He watched the foaming specks of light until his eyes hurt. At first, the weight of the universe pressed down on his chest until he could scarcely breathe, and then he was lifted up and he floated toward the stars and he looked back and saw the glowing embers of the fire and his body leaning against the rock, getting smaller and smaller until, like the stars, he was nothing but a infinitesimal speck in the cosmos.

Energy flowed like a river current into his soul, a flow of knowledge and love and understanding. He was a part of the whole, a part of its prairies, its mountains, its trees and grasses and wildflowers and animals and streams and lakes and winds and other peoples, ancient and modern, who discovered the spirit of place. He heard the mystery that whispered in the wind, swept through the grasses, played through the trees, flowed through the streams, a mystery that acknowledged bigness outside oneself.

And then everything became clear.

Chapter 38

He woke to a faint pink glow that silhouetted the eastern mountains. He'd survived the blizzard. It was Monday, the last day to redeem the ranch. Unless he fell while climbing down the cliffs, there would just be enough time to drive to Cora, pick up the cashier's check and get to the courthouse.

He walked into the solstice circle and sat cross-legged at the end of the arrow to celebrate the rising sun. The sky flashed scarlet as the sun exploded from the mountaintop. A great sense of humility swept over him.

He rose and walked to the edge of the cliff. Below and far distant, the ranch began as green meadows, crossed the river and then rose in a series of trees and grass benches to the very top of snow-covered Coulter Mountain. Home.

The two ravens circled overhead and cawed. He raised face and hands toward the sun and felt the aching weight of loneliness lift. Now he had to find his way down the cliffs.

Two hours later, safely below the cliffs, as he walked through a meadow, a horseman, leading another horse, rode out of the distant forest. Still in shadows, the rider was indistinguishable.

He waved and tried to shout, but his throat constricted. He stumbled toward the rider, who disappeared into a small valley. He tripped and fell in grass scented by wildflowers. He was exhausted. He wanted to lie there forever, but he had to get to the courthouse. He struggled to his feet as the rider topped the crest of the meadow. The horse's nostrils flared as it pranced forward. He looked at the rider and thought it was another vision.

Sara's horse snorted and skittered away. She fought for control and finally reined to a stop. She tipped her hat back and smiled. "He doesn't think you smell good. I agree. You're a stinking mess."

"I need to clean up."

"I was sort of worried about you."

"How did you find me?"

"I started looking when you didn't call last night. I stayed at your place. This morning at dawn, I spotted two ravens circling the cliffs above the Indian quest place. I used the binoculars and watched you stand on the edge of the cliff with your arms spread wide open, like you were going to do a swan dive. What were you doing?"

"Giving thanks."

"Because you were lucky?"

"I was blessed."

She handed him the reins of the saddle horse. He put his foot on the stirrup and tried to swing into the saddle. The horse skittered away. He tried again. The horse snorted and reared. He fell to the ground. Sara gathered up the horse, led it back and soothed it while he mounted.

"Do the others know?" he asked.

"I called them to let them know I saw you at the vision quest spot. They are on their way back. I also called the sheriff's office to tell them you were safe and to cancel the search."

"You called the sheriff?"

"Yes, I called to report you missing, but Search and Rescue couldn't get over the pass yesterday. What's wrong?" she asked.

"Nothing really. I was just thinking that the developer and I cut the local banker out of the deal. The developer said I should be careful, because no one knows what someone would do to save millions of dollars."

"He had to be joking," she said.

"Probably."

They rode next to each other in silence for a few minutes.

He reined his horse close to hers. "I'm going back tomorrow."

"I thought so. Your life is in New York. My life is here and San Francisco."

"There are telephones and jets and the Internet."

"Yes, but rumor has it you work all the time."

"I've been working my way to the top, I'm almost there. We could build a new life together. I'll sell my condo and we'll find our own home. You and Will can spend summers here. I'll fly out on weekends."

"How exciting," she said "Does Harry figure into these plans anywhere?"

"Of course. Once I'm settled in my new partnership, I'll hire and mentor him."

"Isn't raising a son and being with the person who loves you and being with your family hold enough meaning?"

"You don't understand," he said.

"I understand. Your life is making money."

"That's not fair!"

"You're still trying to prove your father was wrong about you being worthless," she said. "Let me know when you decide enough is enough."

Chapter 39

Justin returned to his cabin, showered and put on clean clothes. He walked into the living room. Sara waited for him with a thermos of coffee. She insisted on driving to town with him. "We can take my truck."

"The road will be terrible with deep snow. Our 4-wheel drive dump truck has a higher clearance. It's heavier, so we'll have better traction," he said.

They drove her truck to the barn where the dump truck was parked. He looked in the truck's bed and was pleased to see a large slab of foundation rock from the shed. The extra weight would give additional traction.

Sara said, "I have more experience driving the pass than you. I'll drive. Besides, I don't want you to fall asleep and kill us." She jumped into the driver's seat before he could complain.

They drove past the barns, through the pasture and down the road toward Dead Man's Pass.

"I haven't had a girl drive me since high school."

"That was me."

"I knew that."

"Don't forget it."

They rode in silence toward the top of the pass, listening to the tires slice through muddy slush.

"Getting colder."

She switched on the defroster fan to clear a thin film of fog that fringed the edges of the windshield. They hit a pothole. Muddy water splashed over the windshield. She flipped on the wipers and hit the washer.

"Lousy road. Think they would have paved it," he muttered.

"Keeps the motorcycle and RV groupies out of our valley."

He grinned. "Always the optimist."

The truck hit a washboard and fishtailed. She spun the steering wheel and overcompensated. They slid close to the edge and then swerved to the right before she regained control.

"I'd better drop it into four-wheel-drive." She wiped sweaty palms against her jeans before engaging all wheels.

"So far, so good. We'll make it," he said.

The truck plowed through deeper snow on the last curve before the summit. After they passed the pullout to the rock pit at the top of the pass, they heard a siren. The Search and Rescue truck swerved onto the road behind them, spewing mud and snow, strobe lights flashing. The truck gained on them.

Sara braked as she turned into the first downhill switchback.

Justin looked through the rear window. He shouted, "Don't stop!"

"What?"

"That's not the sheriff. That's Kurt Kamm. He wants to stop us from redeeming the mortgage."

Sara took her foot off the brake pedal. "He probably just wants to make certain you're okay."

"We can talk with him at the courthouse. Not here. Keep moving!"

She picked up speed on the short straightaway before the sharp left hand curve that skirted the cliff.

Kamm's truck's grill rammed their bumper, pushing them toward the edge. She accelerated, spun the wheel and brought the truck under control.

The banker's truck bumped them on their left rear bed and

locked solid and then pushed them toward the cliff — it would be over in seconds.

Justin grabbed the dump bed control box and jammed its lever forward. Nothing happened.

The rear of their truck slid to the right, closer to the edge. The trucks separated.

He looked out the back window. "The bed's not rising!"

Sara floored the accelerator to separate the vehicles.

Justin was holding the control box upside down, just like Will had done when they dumped the shed debris into the pit. He pulled the lever toward him. The truck bed began to rise as the killer gunned to ram them again. Life couldn't end here — he didn't want to die like his old man. He didn't want to die with Sara — he wanted to live with her. And most of all, he didn't want his son to be an orphan.

He looked through the rear window. The slab of rock hadn't budged. He jiggled the lever to try to speed up the lift of the bed. The weight shift was subtle, almost imperceptible at first, and then the rock accelerated down the bed and then fell between the vehicles. It wedged under the banker's front axle. Kamm accelerated and his grill guard hit their rear and pushed them closer to the edge.

The rock slab lifted Kamm's front tires inches off the road. He lost steering. Panicked, he jammed the accelerator to the floor. He slid through the mud and snow toward the edge.

Sara's right rear tire slipped over the edge. Their truck tipped. Justin gripped the dashboard and ceiling.

She slammed the gas pedal to the floor. The front tires, engaged in four-wheel drive, dug through the mud onto solid ground and pulled the truck back onto the road.

Crazed, Kurt Kamm spun his steering wheel and slammed on his brakes as his truck skidded toward the edge of the cliff. His front tires slipped over and the rock slab, freed from the friction between the truck's axle and muddy road, tumbled into space and out of sight. The Search and Rescue truck settled with a thump, balanced on its frame on the edge of the cliff. Its front hung in air, its hood tilted slightly downward. It balanced on the cliff. The banker stared at huge boulders hundreds of feet below and strangled the steering wheel.

Justin and Sara jumped out of their truck.

Kurt Kamm took his hands from the steering wheel. The truck gently rocked. He screamed for help. His Stetson fell off.

"Hold on! Don't move. We'll pull you back." Justin grabbed the logging chain from behind the dump truck's front seat and wrapped it around the back frame's ball hitch and then secured it by slipping a link through the grab hook.

"Sara, watch this. Don't let it slip off!"

He grabbed the other end of the chain and ran toward the rear of Kamm's truck to attach it to that ball hitch.

Kamm watched him run toward his truck. "You aren't going to push me over the edge. I'll kill you first!" He pulled a semi-automatic and swung his arm over the seat to shoot Justin through the back window. The shot shattered the window and went high. The truck tipped. Kamm screamed. The truck slid off the cliff and plummeted out of sight.

Still gripping the chain, Justin ran to the edge and watched the truck tumble end-over-end through space. Finally, after what seemed an eternity, it smashed onto the boulders far below.

Sara ran to Justin and looked down. The truck settled deeper against the rocks, creating a myriad of sparks. Gas spilled from the two spare gas cans. It ignited. Rivulets of flames snaked around the truck body.

"It's going to blow," he said.

"That only happens in the movies."

"It'll go."

"I can't watch." She walked back toward their truck.

The gas tank exploded in an orange-red flash and the sound

boomed off the cliffs. He felt the shock wave. There was a slight tremor of the earth beneath him. The edge caved in. Justin fell off the cliff.

Falling, he gripped the chain hard. His body wrenched to a stop when the chain tightened against the truck's hitch. He swung like a pendulum. He heard Sara scream. He twisted toward the bank, hoping to use his feet to scramble back up, but the cave-in had carved the side concave - he couldn't reach the bank.

She looked over the edge. "I'll pull you up."

He felt her useless tugs against his dead weight.

"You're too heavy," she cried.

"Use the truck!"

He was exhausted. He slipped down the chain link by link. Seven feet of chain remained before he'd fall. He didn't have the strength to stop himself. The truck's engine started. The truck jerked forward and he slid two feet further down the chain. Sweat ran down his forehead. His eyes stung. He smelled his own rank odor. Another foot of chain links slid through raw fingers.

He looked down. Several feet of chain remained before he'd plunge to his death. The grab hook swung near his thigh. One chance. He loosened his grip on the chain and slid down until the point of the grab hook was just below his leather belt. He twisted and then he lowered himself onto it. The point slipped under his belt. He slid down the chain until he was hooked solid.

Sara pulled him up to the safety of the road. They sat in the truck panting for breath.

"Kurt Kamm tried to kill us," she said.

"Gordon was right. Some people will do anything for money."

"How did Kurt know you'd be driving over the pass?"

"Today's the deadline and when he heard I survived the blizzard, he came up here and waited. I remember seeing the dispatcher's radio in his office and then that truck parked in the bank lot. Kamm was a first responder for Search and Rescue, so he had a radio and the truck. He probably killed my father the same way. Cody said there were unusual tire tracks at the scene."

"Do you think the sheriff was involved in Kamm's plan?" she asked.

"My investigator didn't find anything to link them. It's a small town, the sheriff and the banker worked together on volunteer projects. Billy has a big mouth and he's full of himself, but I don't think he's dishonest."

"What now?" she asked.

"It's a crime to leave the scene of an accident, but there's nothing we can do for Kamm. He couldn't have survived. No one will drive past and if they do, they won't see the wreckage."

"They'll see the smoke."

"Not for long. The wind will disperse it. It'll burn out. We'll drive to town. You phone in an accident report after I redeem the mortgage."

"What should I say?" she asked.

"Tell the truth. We saw Kamm lose control. We tried to save him, but it was too late."

"You're a mess. I'll buy you a new shirt and Levis. You can change in the truck before going to the courthouse," she said.

"That's why I need you around."

Chapter 40

That evening, when they returned to the ranch, Otto leapt off the porch, ran to greet Sara and then growled at Justin. When they walked into the cabin, Linda, Will and Cody sat at the table. They looked up at them.

Cody tipped back in his chair. "Sara called and told us about your adventure. You okay?"

"I survived. Lost Jake." Justin poured himself a cup of coffee and joined them.

"You redeem the mortgage?" Cody's voice was tight.

"Got to the courthouse just in time," Justin said.

"Sell it to the fucking developer?"

Justin took a paper from his back pocket and slid it across the table to Cody.

Cody gave him a quizzical look and then opened the paper and read.

"This ain't right."

"What's wrong?"

"This deed is made out to me and Linda. Thought you signed a contract with that developer," Cody said.

"The developer had signed the agreement. I was supposed to sign it today. I tore it up."

"Won't he be pissed?"

"Yes, he will be really upset, but he's a businessman, he understands a deal is not done until the last "t" has been crossed. There's nothing he can do legally other than file a suit to harass me, but it won't hold up. After fighting that blizzard, that developer means nothing to me."

"How come you changed your mind?"

"I had time to think things over when I was stranded up on the vision quest place."

Cody sat for a moment. "Thanks."

They nodded at each other. That said there wasn't anything more needed saying.

Linda got up and hugged Justin.

"I discovered a special place where Dad would like his ashes spread. I'm leaving for New York tomorrow, but I'll come back later in the summer and we can ride up there and have a ceremony."

"Leaving tomorrow?" Linda said.

"I don't want to go!" Will said.

Linda put her hand on the boy's arm. "Cody and I'd like him to stay the summer with us."

"He'll have to come back for school," Justin said.

"Why? He can go to Cora if he wants," Cody said.

"He needs a good education," Justin said.

"Seems like you done all right here in Cora," Cody said.

"You'd have to drive him every day."

"Our old man done it. And when we was old enough, we drove."

"Please, Dad," Will said.

Justin turned to Cody. "What would you think about closing this place up and moving to town for the winter?"

Cody looked at Linda.

"It would be nice to get out of the winters up here. But we can't afford to rent a place in town," she said.

"You could stay at Miss Adams' house. Needs airing out and a little paint, but it's available, rent free," Justin said.

"Wouldn't make much difference — I've have to drive up here every day to feed the stock," Cody said.

"I could rent winter pasture close to town," Justin said.

Cody looked at his brother and then smiled. "Then it's settled."

"Not yet. Let's make that decision at the end of the summer. See how Will feels about it at that time. I'll come back in August and we'll talk about it. Is that all right with you, Will?"

"Insane!"

Justin walked Sara out to her truck. He was exhausted. There was nothing more he could think of to persuade her to join him in Manhattan. He kissed her.

"Come back with me. Marry me." he said. "I think I've proved I'm not just about the money."

"I love you, I love what you did in there, but I love this place, too, and I'm not made for Manhattan. That doesn't mean we can't be special friends."

He kissed her goodbye and savored the scent of her hair. She got into her truck and he watched her taillights disappear down the long gravel driveway.

He walked to the cabin and up the stairs to his old room. Will was reading in bed. He sat on the bed. "I'm going to miss you, son."

Will frowned. "I guess I'll miss you, too."

He reached into his pocket and pulled out his river stone and told his son its story. "It's brought me good luck and I'd like you to have it so you'll remember me."

"Gee, thanks." Will took the stone, turned it over in his fingers and looked at it.

"I want you to remember I love you, Will." He kissed his son's forehead and hugged him and then walked to the door and looked back. Will was turning the river stone over, watching the color change in the lamplight.

He was half way down the stairs when he realized he'd told

his son the same thing his mother had told him the night before she disappeared.

Chapter 41

Before dawn, Justin drove the rental car down the driveway, past the barns and through the ranch gate. He followed yesterday's dump truck tracks through the snow over Dead Man's Pass. On the highway to Missoula, he talked on his cell phone with his assistant, making arrangements. Upon his return to the city, he planned to hit the ground running — pay off Farnsworth's loan and sign the partnership agreement with Duncan. Several hours later, he boarded his private jet and it taxied toward the take-off runway.

The jet screeched to a halt. His briefcase slid off the seat across the aisle and onto the floor. Justin watched a single engine plane taxi past a few feet in front of his jet.

The cockpit door opened and the co-pilot said, "Sorry about that abrupt stop. A student pilot cut right in front of us."

"Student pilot?" Justin asked.

The co-pilot laughed. "Yeah, he's on his first cross-country solo. From the sound of his voice on the radio, he's scared to death. We're going to let him clear the area and then we'll be on our way."

A few minutes later, Justin's jet taxied to Runway 29, accelerated and then rotated for take-off. Cumulus clouds massed to the north. The cloud base was depressing black, the white tops churned upward, penetrating the blue sky as if propelled by an explosion.

The pilot swung around the storm and the jet leveled out in smooth air, flying east at 500 knots.

Justin looked out the window at the clouds. He imagined joining Duncan's firm, structuring huge deals, sitting at lead tables at charity events, basking in the respect of others, knowing his life was productive and it served a purpose. He would make things happen that enriched society. And he would get even richer in the process. His life in the city would be a continuation of his previous life. He knew what to expect. That life would be predictable. He was a player in the city. No, he was more than a player — as Duncan's partner, he would become the leader of all the players. He would be Justin Thatcher, King of the Mountain. He smiled.

He leaned back against the soft leather seat, closed his eyes and drifted into a dream.

He said goodbye to Will, Sara and Cody and walked away through a meadow of vibrant grasses and fragrant wildflowers. The sun warmed his back, but he walked into a cold wind and, in the far distance, darkness obscured his goal. As he walked further from his family, the grass under his feet began to die, the flowers wilt. The grass grew brittle and snapped off under his footsteps until the ground became barren, littered with rocks. The sky turned ugly. The wind kicked up dust devils that whirlpooled the earth up into a dark mass. His feet grew heavier. Every step carried him closer to the old loneliness. He had made a mistake. He wanted to return. Sara's voice called from the distance, a faint warning.

He turned. The bear crouched between him and his family. Its head swung from side to side, white spittle flew from its massive jaws. As Justin watched, the bear stood on hind feet, front claws ripping the air.

He thought he had gotten rid of the bear when he destroyed the shed, but now he knew he had to live the rest of his life with his nightmare beast. It stood in the way of what he wanted. This horrid dance had to stop, one way or another. Using both hands, he picked up a watermelon sized boulder and held it high over his head. He began walking toward the bear. The beast dropped to all fours, growled and bared its fangs. Justin kept walking toward the bear. It charged. Justin waited until the beast was upon him and then he flung the boulder with all his strength against the bear's massive head. There was a hollow thump. The bear's evil black eyes stared at Justin for a long moment and then the beast's body began to fracture, then pixelate, until the body dissolved into dust. His nightmare bear would never threaten him again. He ran toward his family and his entire being filled with joy. He shouted their names . . .

Disoriented, Justin woke from the dream, using the back of his hand to wipe sleep-drool from his chin, the wetness waking him further and magnifying the empty feelings now pouring through his body. Alone, he looked through the window at the jet's shadow tearing across white clouds, knowing his life was like that shadow, knowing there was no permanence, knowing he could return to Manhattan to become King of the Mountain. But kings come and go. Only the mountains endure.

He replayed the dream from its beginning — leaving Sara, Will and Cody behind, turning toward a sterile future, confronting and destroying the bear and then returning to his family, feeling a rush of joy. He'd broken his vow to never return to the ranch and in doing so he reconciled with his past, understanding his relationship with his father, discovering he was not who he thought he was, connecting with his son and, seeing through the boy's eyes the land and its people in a new light, discovering he had another son, Harry, a fine young man, and best of all, reconnecting with his first love, the only love he would ever know.

The dream gave urgency to his new feelings and in this swiftly moving jet he began to understand there would be no meaning to his life without his family, no meaning without friendships and laughter.

He knew with an unshakeable clarity that no amount of money could take him there or buy the mystical oneness he'd experienced at the spirit circle, where he'd merged with the stars, when everything had become clear.

Hands trembling, he opened his briefcase and took out a pad of paper and wrote down a name and phone number. Then, with a deep breath, and with the sureness of his biggest financial victory in Manhattan, he unbuckled his seatbelt and walked up the aisle to the cockpit. He handed the note to the pilot and said, "Take me back to the airport. Have the tower call and tell Sara I'm coming home."

Acknowledgements

The theme of *River Stone* germinated when University of Colorado Chancellor Richard Byyny introduced me to Archbishop Desmond Tutu. Archbishop Tutu told me, "You have to reconcile with the past, before you can move into the future."

New York Times best selling author Doug Looney gave me encouraging advice, as did Barbara Steiner, author of over 70 novels.

My friend and fellow author Bob Morgan was always there to critique another idea, another passage, another paragraph, another chapter, again and again and again, always with honesty, humor and patience.

Manhattan's Renee and Joel Klaperman invited us for lunch at the Harvard Club so I could describe the Harvard Hall scene. Renee also read several draft chapters.

I tested ideas and received feedback from experts in various fields: my friend and mentor Charlie Butcher, who taught me not to live solely for the expectations of others; Dr. John Sadler for nightmares caused by abuse; Lewis House, Ph.D., for intelligence gathering; Don Trieschmann for business deal stories; Aylife Ris and Sara Caile for spirituality themes; Charlie Winsor for speech patterns of eleven-year-olds; Susan Borst and Caroline Arman for insights into the way women Sara's age think, and Jane Butcher for her reading an early draft, her ideas and her unwavering encouragement. Jeff Limerick and Shirley Sudow read early drafts and offered their feedback.

My friend Nic Patrick and I shared twenty-seven years exploring the backcountry of the Yellowstone ecosystem.

He, along with Mike Bromley, Fred Eichler and Troy Barnett, helped me better understand our connection to the land and its creatures.

Artist Jack Thompson shared creative insights. Alan Rudy's dinner party reading of *Eulogy for a Bear,* from my earlier book, *Love of the Hunt,* gave me confidence to bear down (pardon the pun) and finish *River Stone.*

Thanks to the rest of my Coffee Group: Paul Bauman, Stewart Hoover, Mike Maloy, Fred Ris, Ron Stewart and Andy Skumancih, for your courteous expressions of interest and for not rolling your eyes when I described certain scenes.

Authors Jerrie Hurd, Kurt Gutjar, and Kathleen Phillips were incredibly helpful with their ideas and edits to the manuscript. I am deeply indebted to my editor K.T. Roes for her wisdom and insights.

My wife, Tish, played a major role with her encouragement, her advice and her insight into plot and characters. And thanks to John, Susan and Tom for their interest and confidence that, finally, their old man would finish his novel.

So, thanks to all of you who have listened with good humor and endless patience during my struggle to better understand the characters in this novel. Those characters, like good friends, revealed their innermost thoughts, desires, fears and motivations slowly. I'm blessed to have so many friends who helped me shape *River Stone* that I'm fearful that I've forgotten to thank *you* specifically. If I did forget you, let me know. I'll buy you a beer and then let you choose a name for a character in my next story.

- JB Winsor